"Is That What This Is All About? To Slow Me Down?"

"No, Darby. This is all about stopping you."

He shifted his stance. His hand brushed hers, and they both froze. The attraction between them was suddenly palpable. His eyes went dark, and she realized that at any other time, and with any other man in this circumstance, she'd be tilting her head up for a kiss.

But instead of kissing her, he spoke, his voice a low, sexy rumble. "I seriously want to kick your butt."

She couldn't seem to stop the mocking smile that formed on her lips. "No, you don't, Seth. You seriously want to kiss my mouth. Admit it," she cajoled.

To her surprise, he immediately swooped in.

* * *

A Cowboy's Temptation
is a Colorado Cattle Barons novel:

From the mountains to the boardroom, these men have everything under control—except their hearts

* * *

If you're on Twitter,
tell us what you think of Harlequin Desire!
#harlequindesire

D0043496

NOV 13

Dear Reader,

Welcome to *A Cowboy's Temptation,* book five of the Colorado Cattle Barons series from Harlequin Desire. It's been two years since I started writing about the Jacobs and Terrell families, and I've found myself falling in love with the rugged men and intrepid women of Lyndon Valley.

Now that his three sisters are married off, it's cowboy Seth Jacobs's turn to meet the woman of his dreams. Former army captain Darby Carroll is as independent as they come. The last thing she needs messing up her well-ordered life and plans for her bucolic Lyndon Valley retreat is Seth and his treasured railway. He might be tough, but she'll take him on and shut him down, no matter what it takes. Oh, and of course, fall in love, too!

I hope you enjoy *A Cowboy's Temptation.*

Happy reading!

Barbara Dunlop

A COWBOY'S TEMPTATION

—

BARBARA DUNLOP

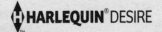

HARLEQUIN® DESIRE

Recycling programs
for this product may
not exist in your area.

ISBN-13: 978-0-373-73274-6

A COWBOY'S TEMPTATION

Printed in U.S.A.

www.Harlequin.com

Books by Barbara Dunlop

Harlequin Desire

An After-Hours Affair #2108
ΔA Cowboy Comes Home #2134
ΔA Cowboy in Manhattan #2140
ΔAn Intimate Bargain #2158
A Golden Betrayal #2198
A Conflict of Interest #2204
ΔMillionaire in a Stetson #2224

Silhouette Desire

Thunderbolt over Texas #1704
Marriage Terms #1741
The Billionaire's Bidding #1793
The Billionaire Who Bought Christmas #1836
Beauty and the Billionaire #1853
Marriage, Manhattan Style #1897
Transformed Into the Frenchman's Mistress #1929
*Seduction and the CEO #1996
*In Bed with the Wrangler #2003
*His Convenient Virgin Bride #2009
The CEO's Accidental Bride #2062
Billionaire Baby Dilemma #2073

*Montana Millionaires: The Ryders
ΔColorado Cattle Barons

Other titles by this author available in ebook format.

BARBARA DUNLOP

writes romantic stories while curled up in a log cabin in Canada's far north, where bears outnumber people and it snows six months of the year. Fortunately she has a brawny husband and two teenage children to haul firewood and clear the driveway while she sips cocoa and muses about her upcoming chapters. Barbara loves to hear from readers. You can contact her through her website, www.barbaradunlop.com.

For my daughter, with love.

One

He didn't look much like a mayor—especially in the lighted ranch yard, wearing blue jeans and a battered Stetson, his dark eyes, square chin and straight nose set in a deeply tanned face. From this distance, Seth Jacobs was all cowboy, all rugged and as powerful as they came in Lyndon Valley.

Sipping her vodka tonic out of a disposable plastic cup, Darby Carroll hovered in the wide-open doorway of the newly raised Davelyn barn. Thirty feet across the dirt construction site, Seth was standing with a group of cowboys, chatting over an open fire, passing around a bottle of Jack Daniel's whiskey. He chuckled at something one of the cowboys said, white teeth flashing in the firelight.

It was nearing ten at night, and most of the young Lyndon Valley families had packed up their kids and headed for home. The holdouts were the singles, young married couples and a few fiftysomethings, whose child-rearing days were over, but who hadn't yet traded after-parties for early bedtimes and cups of hot tea.

The September sky was awash with stars, muted dance

music throbbing far behind her. The air was warm, fragrant with wheatgrass, and the Lyndon River roared softly at the base of the hill. Most of the west valley had shown up for the barn raising. Community was alive and well in Lyndon.

Family was everything. And that only added to Seth's power and prestige. While the Jacobses had arrived many generations ago, Darby was a newcomer, having taken over her estranged great-aunt's property only three years previous. There were people who thought she wasn't entitled to an opinion, many who thought the old guard should remain in charge forever. She took another sip of the tart, bracing drink, gaze still resting on the group of six cowboys.

She couldn't help but wonder if an in-person appeal would help her cause. She had so much to say to him, so many points to make, arguments to mount, facts and figures to put forward. That is, if Seth Jacobs or anyone else was willing to listen.

He caught her gaze, trapping her in place as surely as if he'd wrapped his callous hands around her arms and held her steady. He cocked his head, spoke to the cowboy next to him, handed over the bottle then broke from the group, pacing toward her.

His shoulders were wide, hips slim, strides easy as he ate up the ground between them. She had no doubt whatsoever that he'd garnered nearly 100 percent of female voters in the mayoral election. Well, maybe 99.9, since Darby had voted for his opponent.

He slowed his pace, stopping in front of her in the doorway. "You look like a woman who has something to say."

She brushed her auburn hair behind her shoulders. "Are you a man who's willing to listen?"

"I took an oath that says I am," he responded easily, shifting to lean one shoulder against the wide jamb of the barn doorway. "I take it doubly serious for pretty women."

"I'm not here to flirt with you, Mayor."

There was a teasing warmth in his dark, blue eyes. "Too bad."

"I'm here to argue with you."

He heaved a sigh. "Yeah, well, that's my bad luck, too."

"Did you know that a train whistle is one hundred thirty to one hundred fifty decibels?"

"Can't say that I did," he drawled.

"At one hundred twenty-five decibels, pain begins." She tugged at her ear as she quoted the researched statistics. "At one hundred forty decibels, even short-term exposure can cause permanent damage."

"You know, you have the most arresting eyes. What are they, turquoise? Green?"

Darby's thoughts stumbled for a split second. But she reminded herself that it was the Jack Daniel's and the cowboy talking. She had to focus on the mayor.

"Right now, we're talking about my ears."

He smiled at that, canting his head to one side. "Interesting ears, too."

"And I'd like to keep them in working order. Mine and those of every other resident of Lyndon Valley, especially the children."

"Well, unless you're planning to stand on the tracks, I'm guessing your ears will be safe."

She ignored his sarcasm. "Uncontrolled railway crossings account for eighty-nine percent of fatal train-vehicle collisions."

"Again, my advice is to keep your pretty eyes, your pretty ears—" he drew slightly back to make a show of checking out the length of her body "—and your pretty little body off the railway tracks."

"How drunk are you?" she asked, wondering if there was any reason to continue the conversation.

He grinned unrepentantly. "Why?"

"Because you're not behaving much like a mayor."

"My mistake."

He removed his Stetson, raking his fingers through his hair to give it some semblance of order. He squared his shoulders and neutralized the cocky grin. "Better?"

"Your draft plan calls for twelve uncontrolled railway crossings in the greater Lyndon City area."

"Yes," he agreed.

"That's twelve new chances for Lyndon City citizens to die."

"You don't think they'll notice the one-hundred-thirty-decibel whistle and get out of the way?"

Darby was not going to be deterred. "That adds up to twelve blasts, per train, of up to one hundred fifty decibels, twenty-four hours a day, seven days a week."

His grin crept back. "You did the math."

"I did the math. And you need to take this seriously."

"Mountain Railway is pouring tens of millions of dollars into the region. Believe me when I tell you I take that kind of money very seriously."

She polished off the last of her drink. "Money's not everything."

"The railway benefits the ranchers and other businesses, such as DFB Brewery, and it brings new economic opportunities to the entire region," he countered, not seeming remotely intoxicated now.

Darby did some other math inside her head. Perhaps three vodka tonics into the evening wasn't the best time to get into this debate.

But Seth wasn't finished. "Ranchers and trains have been coexisting in this country for well over two hundred years."

"There are more than just ranchers living in Lyndon Valley."

He smiled again, knowingly this time. "And there we have it. The crux of your opposition. You think the ambiance at your ladies' retreat should take precedence over the economic well-being of the Lyndon City ranching community."

"My *ladies' retreat?*" Darby felt her cheeks heat with indignation on behalf of her clientele. "Do you think we're up there quilting and swapping cookie recipes?"

"What are you doing up there?"

What they were doing up there was none of his business, and she had no intention of sharing it with him. It wasn't exactly a state secret, but there were definitely elements of national security.

"Fair warning, Mayor Jacobs. I'm going to formally request you hold a referendum on whether or not to allow a railway line through Lyndon Valley," she told him instead.

His smirk telegraphed to her he'd noted the evasion. "I don't need a referendum. The new railway line was the centerpiece of my campaign."

"That's why I voted for Hal Jameson."

Seth gave an unconcerned shrug. "Yet, I won."

"That doesn't mean you get to be a tyrant."

"They voted *with* me on the issue, Darby. You're in the minority. That's how democracy works."

She leaned a little closer to him. "Democracy also gives me the right to free speech."

He searched her expression for a full minute. Was he impressed, annoyed, refocusing and coming at it from a new angle? She couldn't help but wonder if she'd made her point.

"You really do have incredible eyes," he said.

The unexpected statement caused a little lurch of attraction inside her chest, but she quickly shoved it to the far reaches of her being. "Behave yourself, Mayor Jacobs."

"Free speech, Ms. Carroll. It works both ways."

"Are you telling me your mayor's code of conduct allows you to flirt with the citizens?"

"I'm not on the job right now. I'm attending a party."

She had to concede that point to him. "Then we should stop talking business."

She hated to admit it, but maybe this hadn't been the greatest idea.

"You started it. I wanted to flirt all along."

She held her ground. "I'll never flirt back."

"Too bad for me."

"Mayor," she warned, not liking his apparent knack for flirting, nor how susceptible she appeared to be to it. "I'm your opposition."

"On a single issue."

"It's do or die for me."

"It's do or die for me, too." He gave a regretful shake of his head. "But you still have astonishing eyes."

She ignored his attempt at distraction and refused to be swayed. At the same time, she used a warning tone. "That's not the only thing I have."

Darby had a Ph.D. in psychology, a black belt in karate and five years' experience in the military. Normally, she was prepared for any challenge, but she'd never run up against politics before. And she'd never run up against anyone like Seth Jacobs.

Just by walking into a room, he seemed to garner respect in Lyndon City. People spoke about him with awe, and she'd yet to meet anyone willing to fight him head-on. He was a unique and formidable opponent, and he was standing between her and her dream.

Arriving at her home, Sierra Hotel, she left her SUV in the front driveway and made her way into the entry lounge. A new group of guests was expected late next week, but for now, she and her small staff had the lakefront retreat to themselves.

"How'd it go?" asked Marta Laurent. Marta had been her first friend in Lyndon Valley, and she was now assistant manager at Sierra Hotel. Marta muted a news story on the widescreen television. "Did you get a chance to talk to him?"

Darby dropped her small backpack on the end of a sofa and plunked herself down. "I did. But I don't think he's taking me seriously. Hey, have you noticed anything weird about my eyes?"

"There's nothing wrong with your eyes. What did he say?"

"He said the Lyndon City constituents put him into office knowing he was in favor of the railway, so he doesn't need a referendum now."

"He's not wrong about that," Marta conceded with her usual logic.

"I know," Darby had to agree. "He's wrong to support the railway. But he's not wrong to say people knew about it when they elected him."

"Did you check? Is there any way to force him to hold a referendum?"

"The only way to do it is to get six hundred signatures on a petition by next Monday."

"That's not impossible," Marta mused, sitting up straighter. "I know a lot of people. We can canvass the city, mount a public-information campaign, put clipboards at sympathetic businesses."

"Fight politics with politics?" Darby couldn't help but let her optimism rise.

She'd do anything to protect Sierra Hotel. She loved this place, and she knew it provided a vital service to women.

On the shores of Berlynn Lake, it was in a perfect retreat location for women who worked in high-intensity, male-dominated security, defense and law-enforcement jobs. Here, they could recharge and rejuvenate around others who understood the pressures of their careers. One of the things they needed to get away from was sudden, loud noises.

As a military psychologist, she'd been frustrated by the narrow range of support options she could provide to female soldiers in combat. They didn't want to engage in the typical R & R activities that their male counterparts used to blow off steam. The women needed camaraderie, a safe place to let their hair down and interact with peers. And so, Sierra Hotel was born.

Darby had put everything she had into building it, including taking out a rather sizeable mortgage on the land, resulting in payments that she was only just able to maintain. Luckily, word was spreading, and her client base was growing.

She came to her feet, drawn toward the big window and the soothing view beyond, her large back deck, a rolling lawn, a pot-lighted pathway leading to a sandy beach.

"We can't let this happen," she said out loud.

Marta followed her lead, coming to stand next to her in front of the glass. "We won't."

"They've been trucking steers from Lyndon Valley to the railhead for decades," Darby reasoned, framing up a new tactic. "Ranching has been profitable so far. This railroad is only a matter of convenience."

"Whereas Sierra Hotel is irreplaceable," Marta added. "With far-reaching implications to the safety and security of our nation. Why don't you tell the mayor what you do up here? That might help him understand."

Darby shook her head. "We can't call that kind of attention to ourselves."

Some of her clients were high-value targets of the country's enemies. Many were irreplaceable to their organizations. And most represented an investment of millions of dollars in their personal recruitment and training. Clustering them together required a certain level of secrecy and discretion.

"Yeah, I get that," said Marta.

"We have to stop the railway development without giving ourselves away."

"I can have an anti-railway website up and running for us in an hour," Marta offered. "Stop-the-evil-railroad.com."

"Too on the nose," Darby returned, buying into the idea. "Save-our-pristine-wilderness.org."

"Stop-noise-pollution-in-Lyndon."

"That one's not bad." Darby nodded her agreement.

A website was certainly a good place to start. Lyndonites couldn't make the right decision if they didn't have accurate information. At the very least, she had to convince them that holding a referendum was in everybody's best interest. What was the point of democracy if the majority didn't get a chance to make decisions?

"We can put all your facts and figures out there," said Marta. "Charts, graphs, you name it. And we can print up flyers and deliver them door to door. We could target the women close to him in his life. His parents moved away when they retired, but his sisters are in town. Abigail's pregnant."

Darby couldn't help but admire the way Marta's mind worked. It didn't matter what the topic, she automatically cataloged, reviewed, analyzed and predicted.

"You mean pregnant with a baby who might one day get hit by a train," Darby continued the thought.

"Or whose delicate little eardrums might be ruptured by one hundred fifty decibels of train whistle."

"Doesn't his sister Mandy have a baby boy?"

"One year old now."

Darby surprised herself with a grin. "Those are some really great ideas."

"Thanks." Marta smiled in return.

"Seth Jacobs, here we come."

Seth was beginning to realize he might have underestimated Darby Carroll. It was obviously a bias on his part, one he'd never admit to his sisters or his cousin, but it hadn't occurred to him that a woman so incredibly gorgeous and sexy would also be so incredibly efficient.

Staring at the glossy anti-railway poster on the bulletin board in the front office of City Hall, he couldn't help remembering her at the Davelyns' barn raising. Those eyes had been her most startling feature, wide and deep green, lashes dark. But they were by no means the only thing that made her beautiful. Her skin was creamy smooth. She had a sleek mane of auburn hair that cascaded partway down her back. And her compact body seemed as toned and healthy as they came. She gave the impression of coiled energy, like she might spring to action at any moment.

He reached out and tugged the poster down, gazing at the breadth of her handiwork. It was outrageous and impressive at the same time, encouraging Lyndon citizens to demand a referendum.

"I don't think you're allowed to do that," said Lisa Thompson, arriving at his right shoulder. Lisa was his cousin, advisor and chief of staff.

"It's my bulletin board," Seth returned.

"It's the city's bulletin board," she corrected. "And citizens are permitted to post notices for seven days."

"Not when it's hate speech."

She scoffed out a laugh. "It's perfectly legal to hate the railroad."

Reluctantly accepting her argument, he handed Lisa the poster. She waggled her finger in an obvious reprimand of his behavior.

"We've had a dozen more phone calls on the topic this morning," she told him as she repegged it to the large corkboard.

"For or against?"

"A mixed bag. Darby Carroll may well get enough signatures for the referendum. You have to admire the woman's tenacity."

"Tenacity is not exactly what I'm looking for in a woman." Seth would hardly call it her best feature.

"Excuse me?" Lisa raised her brows. "Did I detect a note of sexism there?"

"Stand down, cousin," Seth quickly backpedaled. "I'm not looking for it in a man, either."

"Do I need to reinstate our gender sensitivity lessons?"

"No. Please, no." Raised on the range, Seth was hardly the most enlightened of males, but he could be politically correct when it was required.

"I was thinking you're a lot alike," Lisa observed.

"Who's a lot alike?"

"You and Darby Carroll."

"*Excuse* me?"

She took a step backward. "Don't shoot the messenger, boss. But you have been known to take a stand on certain subjects and flatly refuse to back down."

"I do for the good of the city. And the railway is absolutely for the good of the city."

"I don't disagree."

"Then why are we arguing?"

"I'm only saying she's a worthy adversary."

Seth didn't need a worthy adversary, particularly not a beautiful one with distracting green eyes. He needed a little smooth sailing.

He'd been mayor for nearly a year now, and he'd discovered there were opponents to literally *every* initiative. And it was always the craziest of his detractors who took the time and trouble to call City Hall or write to the newspaper. He swore he couldn't change the toilet paper color in the men's room without a barrage of resistance.

"How long until the rail right-of-way permits are in place?" he asked Lisa.

"The public has one more week to comment."

His attention went back to the poster. "And if she gets enough signatures on the petition?"

"Then it takes sixty days to hold a referendum. That will delay execution of the permits."

Seth could see all his well-placed plans blowing up in his face. "Has anyone been in touch with Mountain Railway? Have they heard about this?"

"I talked with the president yesterday," Lisa said.

"And?"

"And, on the one hand, they're used to these kinds of protests. On the other hand, they're beginning to think this particular protest has legs. And they weren't expecting it."

"Should I call and try to reassure him?" Seth asked.

Lisa shook her head. "Not yet."

"If Darby gets the six hundred signatures?"

"Then you should definitely call him."

"Just once," Seth complained as they made their way up the marble staircase toward his private offices, "just once, I'd like something to be easy."

"Oh, poor boss," she mocked as they walked side by side. "Did you expect them to love you?"

"I expected them to be sane."

"Why would you expect that? You were here during the election campaign."

Seth cracked a smile at that observation. "I know the vast majority of the citizens of Lyndon are smart, reasonable, hard-working people. Why can't any of those ones ever write, call or come out to meetings?"

"They're busy working and raising their families. They're expecting you to run the city for them. That's why they pay you."

He cut through the executive reception area and into his private office. The room was big and airy. A bay window arched out on one side, overlooking the river and the town square. The riverbanks were a little muddy from a recent storm and flood, but the fall colors were brilliant: reds, yellows and greens, stretching their way up the Rocky Mountains.

He moved to the window to take in the view.

Darby was on a ridiculous crusade. A hundred and fifty decibels. The figure was irrelevant. Nobody but the rail-yard workers would be right next to the train when it blew its whistle. And they'd be wearing hearing protection.

Train whistles were hardly newfound, cutting-edge technology that needed to be tested and studied. And the danger of collision was no different here than the danger of collision anywhere else in the country. Lyndon citizens encountered trains as close by as Fern Junction. They all seemed to come back alive.

"Maybe you should talk to her," said Lisa, coming up beside him.

"And say what?"

"Okay, let me rephrase. Maybe you should listen to her."

"You think she'll change my mind?"

Lisa was talking nonsense. She was as much in favor of the railway as anyone else in Lyndon. She'd read the research. She knew what a boon it would be to local businesses.

"Often, people just want to be heard."

"She's being heard all over the damn town." The woman had taken out radio spots.

"She needs to be heard by you," said Lisa.

"No."

"Yes."

"I'm your boss."

"That doesn't mean I'm wrong."

"You are the most insubordinate employee in the world."

She broke into a grin. "I thought we'd established that months ago."

Seth considered her suggestion. "Do you think I made a mistake?"

"In fighting Darby?"

"No, in running for office in the first place."

Part of his rationale for leaving his brother, Travis, to manage the family ranch alone was that from the mayor's seat he'd be able to make the kind of changes the ranching community needed. But so far, all he'd done was get dragged into petty squabbles. Every significant change he'd campaigned on was bogged down in controversy or red tape, or both. Worse still, he was realizing how hard it was to represent the entire city, balance needs, balance agendas. He couldn't simply lobby for the ranchers.

"You're a great mayor," Lisa assured him.

"I wanted to be an effective mayor. I wanted to solve the water-rights issue and get the railway into Lyndon. I wanted to make life better for our neighbors."

"You're doing everything you can."

"It's not enough."

"At least you're trying."

"This isn't third grade. We don't all get a ribbon for showing up."

"Quit wallowing in self-pity."

He arched a brow.

"Cowboy up, Seth. So you've hit a setback. Big deal. What's your next move?"

For about the thousandth time, he found himself capitulating to Lisa's reason. As usual, her initial advice was right.

"I need to talk to Darby Carroll," he admitted.

"You need to *listen* to Darby Carroll."

"That's what I meant."

"Just make sure you remember it during the conversation."

Two

The Valley Fall Festival attracted the who's who of Lyndon Valley. Set in the city's main park next to the river, it was everything from a craft fair and a farmers' market to a family picnic, complete with amateur athletics and fun-filled competitions.

This was Darby's third year attending the event, but today it was about more than just fun. She was chatting with the people, passing out flyers, directing them to the "stop the noise pollution" website and, most important, gathering as many signatures as possible on the petition. Midnight tomorrow was the deadline to file, and they needed nearly a hundred more signatures to guarantee the referendum.

Marta was making her way through the stalls of the farmers' market, while Darby was in the tiny midway, hoping to meet a few concerned mothers putting their children on the merry-go-round and the Ferris wheel.

"A little harder. A little higher," came a deep, familiar, male voice.

Darby twisted her head and spotted Seth Jacobs, perched

on a makeshift platform above a water tank, coaxing the teenage boy who was throwing a baseball at a target to dunk him. The mayor was bone dry so far, and the short lineup of women and preteens looking to take their turn didn't seem to pose much of a threat.

Too bad. She would have loved to see him go under.

She couldn't help musing that it was unfortunate the City Council Chambers didn't have their own dunk tank. The mayor got out of hand at a meeting: boom, down he went.

She smiled at the visual, temptation rising within her.

She knew it would be wrong to give in to her fantasy. This wasn't the time and place to take out her frustration. She had far more important things to do.

Then again, she could afford to blow ten minutes. And if Seth had to head home and change his clothes, she'd have the festival and the citizens all to herself.

It made perfect, strategic sense. Get the adversary out of the way, even if it was only temporarily.

While she talked herself into it, her feet were already taking her toward the dunk tank. She fished into the pocket of her blue jeans and produced a five-dollar bill. For that, the woman at the kiosk handed over three softballs.

Darby was confident she'd only need one.

She took her place in the lineup, fifth back, behind a short, teenage boy who was obviously a friend of the one who'd just failed to hit the target. Behind him were three women, all in heels and dresses, each of them obviously here to flirt with Seth, not to embarrass him.

It didn't take him long to spot her. He glanced to the balls in her hand, and his expression faltered.

She flashed him a confident smile, tossing one of the balls a couple of feet in the air and catching it again with one hand. She knew she shouldn't enjoy this. But there was really no point in fighting her feelings. She felt a buzz of adrenaline come up in anticipation.

He gritted his teeth.

The teenage boy came close but didn't hit the bull's-eye.

The three women all giggled their way through pathetic attempts.

Then it was Darby's turn.

"Mr. Mayor," she greeted.

"Ms. Carroll."

"Ready to get wet?"

"Give it your best shot."

"Oh, I will."

It was far from the first projectile Darby had thrown. She'd played a lot of softball while stationed on bases and overseas. More significant, in basic training, she'd been a great shot with a rifle.

He was wearing a pair of faded blue jeans, sneakers instead of his usual leather boots—probably a good idea—and a blue plaid shirt, with the sleeves rolled up over his tanned forearms.

"You might want to take off your hat," she advised.

"I'll take my chances."

He settled the Stetson more firmly on his head, and their gazes locked.

Adios, Seth Jacobs.

She switched her attention to the target.

"Don't get nervous," he taunted, voice loud and staccato, as if he was trying to psych out a batter. "Don't want to miss. Don't want to choke."

But Darby had spent enough time in a war zone that his shouts weren't going to faze her.

She drew back her arm, pivoted at the elbow and drilled the ball in a straight line.

It hit straight on. The target pinged. The crowd gasped. And Seth's eyes widened a split second before he plunged into the tank.

The crowd squealed and clapped.

"Well, I guess that's it for our brave mayor," came a woman's voice through the tinny loudspeaker. "Round of applause please, ladies and gentlemen. Next up is Carla Sunfall, our very own Miss Wheatgrass."

Darby watched Seth surface. He gave her a fleeting, dark look, before smiling gamely and waving his hat to the crowd. He climbed the ladder out of the tank while two men reaffixed the platform and helped Miss Wheatgrass up to her perch.

Darby turned and handed her spare softballs to the young man behind her.

"Good luck," she told him.

He grinned, likely just as thrilled to have Miss Wheatgrass take the platform as he was to have two extra chances to throw.

Darby left the midway and headed for the baseball field. It had been temporarily turned into a sports track with white paint delineating various lanes and quadrants. There, the organizers were hosting everything from three-legged races to egg tosses. Again, she expected to find mothers with young children who might share her concerns on safety and noise pollution.

"Nice throw," came Seth's voice.

She glanced at him as he drew up beside her, matching her strides. They were out of the main action now, between the backs of the game stalls and a low chain-link fence, where the generators hummed and fans blew heat out of the stalls. The shouts of game players and the electronic buzzes and pings were dampened by the makeshift walls.

"You're looking a little damp, Mr. Mayor."

His shirt was plastered to his broad chest, the soaked fabric delineating the definition of his muscles. His hair was wet, curling darkly across his forehead, and the sheen on his face seemed to accentuate his rugged, handsome features.

Her mouth went dry, and the sun suddenly felt hotter on her head. Her body launched a traitorous rush of hormones, and she didn't dare glance at the fit of his blue jeans.

"All for a good cause," he responded easily, and she couldn't help being disappointed by his equanimity.

He nodded to her clipboard. "How's it going?"

"Almost there."

"Deadline's tomorrow."

"Really?" she drawled. "I hadn't thought to check."

"I wanted to talk to you."

She gazed up and down his body. Oops. Bad idea. He was one sexy specimen of a man. She gave herself a mental shake. "Aren't you going to change your clothes?"

"I've been wet before." His smooth, deep tone added an edge to the comment.

She deliberately ignored it. "It can't be very comfortable."

"I'll live."

"Good to hear. But I'm a little busy right now."

"Did I say talk? I meant I wanted to listen to your side of the situation."

Darby stopped, and Seth stopped, too. She turned to face him, eyes narrowing in suspicion. The old adage that if something seemed too good to be true, it probably was, applied in this case.

"Why?" she asked shortly.

"I'm interested in your concerns."

"No, you're not."

"Then I'm interested in you."

"No," she repeated with finality. "You're not."

"Go ahead. Let's hear your pitch."

"I'm not going to waste my breath." If he gave one whit about her concerns, he'd have listened to them long before now.

"How will you know it's a waste unless you try?" he challenged.

"Let me tell you what I know," she said. "You're worried I might just pull it off. You know I have a lot of signatures, but you're not sure exactly how close I am to six hundred. So 'talking to me' will accomplish one of two things. Either you'll slow me down, making me one, two or ten signatures short *or,* and let me assure you this second one is a very long shot, you'll talk me out of filing the petition."

The expression on his face told her she wasn't wrong.

"I said I wanted to listen," he reminded her.

"Then I'm guessing you're trying option number one. Your intent is to slow me down rather than talk me out of filing."

"I'm not here to slow you down."

"Mr. Mayor—" she canted one hip, resting a hand on her waist "—I believe politicians ought to at least be honest."

She detected a hint of a grin.

"I really do want to listen," he insisted.

"In order to understand me? Or in order to change my mind?"

His expression faltered once more, telling her that seven years of psychology hadn't gone to waste.

"Both," he admitted.

"I admire your honesty, sir."

"You can call me Seth, you know. Everybody does."

"Seth," she repeated, and she saw a slight flare of awareness heat the depths of his eyes.

Uh-oh. Not good. This situation was complicated enough.

Then again… She pulled her thoughts together. Maybe it was something she could use. Maybe she could mess with his focus by pursing her lips or batting her eyelashes. Truly, she'd do anything for the mission.

She tucked her hair behind one ear, moistened her lower lip and subtly pulled her shoulders back, taking on a more provocative pose.

His eyes flared deep blue again, and she knew she was taking the right tack.

A petition, if she actually made the deadline, only got her to the point of a general vote. And winning a general vote meant convincing at least half the town to support her. Might it be easier to change the mind of the one man who could single-handedly stop the railway?

"Okay," she told him. "I'll listen to you."

"Talk to me," he corrected.

"That, too," she agreed.

Seth couldn't recall a sexier woman than Darby Carroll. Which was odd, since she was quite plainly dressed—blue jeans, a white top and a navy blazer. She wasn't wearing a lot of makeup, and she didn't appear to have paid much attention to her hair, simply pulling it back in a jaunty ponytail. A few wisps of auburn curled softly around her temple, but he'd be willing to bet it wasn't on purpose. They'd likely worked their way loose in the breeze.

Her green eyes were clear and intelligent, flecked with gold. Her cheeks were pink, her lips dark and full, and her nose was straight in a perfectly balanced face. She wore a set of tiny blue stones in her ears, but otherwise no jewelry. Not unless he counted her rather large and serviceable watch with its worn leather strap. And he didn't. She couldn't have chosen it to make herself attractive.

They were sitting at a corner table in one of the refreshment tents. She'd surprised him by agreeing to split a syrup-drizzled funnel cake with their coffee, surprised him further by actually tearing off a piece and popping the hot, sticky confection into her mouth.

He couldn't take his gaze off the tiny drop of syrup on her lower lip. Her tongue flicked out to remove it, causing a sharp reaction deep in his gut.

"Decadent," she breathed with a smile, and the sensation hit him again. "Now, what's this all about?"

For a split second, he couldn't remember. Then he dragged himself back to business. This wasn't a date. It was a business meeting. He had to stop thinking like a cowboy and start thinking like the mayor.

"I want to make sure I understand your concerns," he responded, removing a chunk from his own side of the funnel cake. "Why, exactly, do you object so strongly to the railroad?"

She swallowed. "Are you trying to be funny?"

"No."

"It seems like you're making a joke."

"If I was making a joke, one of us would be laughing."

"So I've been white noise for the past three weeks?"

"Excuse me?" This was going to be harder than he'd expected.

"You've pushed everything I've said to the background, ignored me?" She placed the remaining chunk of funnel cake back down to the plate, wiping her fingers on a napkin. "I don't know why that surprises me."

Seth found himself growing impatient. "Do you want to fight with me or talk to me?"

"I want to collect signatures."

"That option wasn't on the list."

Her eyes narrowed. "Do people really let you get away with being such a jerk?"

"Usually, yeah," he admitted, realizing Lisa would be kicking him under the table if she were here. "But give me the benefit of the doubt for a minute. I want to hear what you have to say."

Her green eyes darkened, but her voice went lower, more controlled. "I've told you in every way I know how. Trains are noisy, disruptive and dangerous. They will fundamentally change the character of Lyndon Valley forever."

"For the better," he couldn't help but put in.

She clenched her jaw.

"They'll pass through town, what, three, four, five times a day. For that minor interruption, we'll see enormous immediate benefit and enormous future potential. Mountain Railway is willing to pour tens of millions of dollars into this project, and we'll be the ones who win."

"Is this what you call listening?"

He stopped, regretting he'd defaulted to speech mode. "Sorry." He lifted his cardboard coffee cup and put it to his lips.

"It won't just be three times a day."

He'd allowed it could be four or five, but he stopped himself from pointing that out to her.

"It might be a dozen times a day," she continued. "You know that line is going to eventually link up to Ripple Ridge. They won't be able to resist that link because it cuts nearly two hundred miles off their northwestern interstate. You don't think they'll run their trains over the shortest route possible?"

There was a very likely possibility she was right. But Seth was surprised she'd dug that deep into the company's future possibilities.

"That's not in their plan," was the best he could do as a comeback.

She shot him a look of disbelief. "Please tell me you're capable of connecting the dots."

"Trains run on schedules," he said. "Can't you plan your yoga classes and meditation during a quiet time, maybe do scrapbooking or some basket weaving when a train is due?"

"Gee, I hadn't thought of that," she drawled. "I could organize my life around trains. How tough could that be?"

He stayed silent for a moment, hoping against hope she wasn't being sarcastic.

"Your ranchers are profitable without the railway," she pointed out. "It's a convenience, not a necessity."

"Right back at you," he responded. "Your hotel will survive with a railway. It's a convenience to have one hundred percent peace and quiet, not a necessity."

"It's a necessity."

"Why?" he challenged.

"Women come to Sierra Hotel to get away from loud, sudden noises."

"It upsets their delicate sensibilities?" He knew he was being snarky, but the conversation was getting away from him. He wasn't used to that.

She cracked her first real smile and sat back in her chair. "Yes. My clients have exceedingly delicate sensibilities."

"Maybe they should work on that."

"I'll let them know you said so." She gazed levelly into his eyes.

He got that he had amused her, that there was something she wasn't telling him, but he couldn't for the life of him guess what it was.

"Bottom line, Darby. The train is good for Lyndon."

"Bottom line, Seth. The train is bad for Lyndon."

He gauged the confidence in her expression, realizing what it had to mean, and realizing she was as worthy an adversary as he'd come across in a while. "You've got enough signatures, haven't you?"

"I will have by tomorrow."

"I could arrest you, you know. Have the sheriff lock you up. Hold you overnight on suspicion."

"Suspicion of what?"

He could tell she wasn't taking him seriously.

"Sedition. Rabble-rousing."

She smiled again, shaking her pretty head. "And I could sue you and Lyndon back to the Stone Age."

"You probably could."

"I absolutely could." She picked up the last chunk of the funnel cake before looking him in the eyes. "You're a smart guy, Seth. And you know how to rise to a challenge. You don't have to cheat to get there."

"You're pandering to my ego?" He couldn't help but hope she denied it. And that hope made him realize he wanted her to have a decent opinion of him.

"I'm being honest," she responded.

It was ridiculous, but his chest tightened with some kind of silly pride. "I'm not going to cheat."

That earned him another smile. "Which means I'm going to win."

"Five hundred and ninety-seven," Darby told Marta who was sitting at the computer in the great room at Sierra Hotel. It was eleven-fifty, and they only had ten minutes left to file the petition electronically. "How could we come so close, only to miss?"

They should have worked a little harder, put up a few more posters, run another radio ad, or somehow made their pitch more compelling.

Marta swiveled in the desk chair, her gaze calculating. "If it was me," she began slowly.

Darby waited.

"I'd go ahead and add three more signatures."

"You mean forge them?"

"Nobody real, just scrawl something illegible along the line. I'm sure they'd get lost in the crowd."

"That's illegal. Not to mention immoral."

Marta gave a little shrug. "Risk-benefit analysis. If they double-check each and every signature, they'll throw them out. If they don't, we get a referendum."

"I don't think I could ethically do that." Darby had experienced too many situations where people claimed the end justified the means. It never did.

"Okay, how about this. Six hundred is a lot of signatures to manually count. Are you sure we got it right? Could you have been off by one, maybe two?" She glanced at her watch. "We have seven minutes to file the petition. There's no time for a recount. Are you absolutely, one hundred percent positive on the number?"

Darby thought about it. Okay, that was plausible. How accurate could the true count be?

"I'm sure the people at City Hall are going to double-check when they get it," she cautioned.

"True," Marta agreed. "But if we don't file, it's a definite no. If we do file—" she hovered a finger over the computer keyboard "—we could get lucky. A long shot is better than no shot at all."

"You've scanned all the pages?" Darby asked.

"A few are a bit blurry, making it, you know, maybe a

little hard to get an accurate count." Marta gave her a conspiratorial smile.

"This'll never work," said Darby, even though she was reluctantly smiling back. Could they possibly fudge their way through? Their subterfuge wouldn't make the final decision. It would only give people a chance to vote.

"As a fallback, we'll try for a dozen more signatures tomorrow. I double-checked. The exact wording on the regulation is: 'A petition filed at least twenty-four hours before permit implementation. The petition must be endorsed by at least six hundred residents of Lyndon City.' It doesn't say the six hundred residents must have endorsed it prior to the initial petition filing."

"That has to have been the spirit of the rule," Darby said, coming to her feet to read the screen. Had Marta found a loophole?

"It'll take a judge to say for certain," said Marta. "And, in the meantime, if the railway gets bad press, they might rethink their commitment to the Lyndon Valley route."

Darby moved up behind Marta's chair. "You're frighteningly devious."

"Just thinking things through."

"I'm glad you're on my side."

"I'm always on your side. Here goes nothing." Marta clicked Send on the screen.

They both watched as the cursor flashed across the screen. At eleven fifty-eight, it flashed "Sent."

"Do you suppose he's still up?" asked Darby, picturing Seth in the mayor's mansion. In her imagination, he was in blue jeans and a plaid shirt. She liked him better that way, relaxed and laid-back. When he dressed up in his suit, he seemed to get more uptight.

"I'm sure he's still up," said Marta. "I'm guessing he's swearing a blue streak about now."

Darby found she could easily picture that. "Wine?" she asked, breathing a sigh of temporary relief.

They'd done all they could do for tonight, and she definitely needed to wind down before she tried to sleep.

"Sounds easier than making margaritas," Marta agreed, naming their favorite drink. "You want to do a swim first? I've been either sitting or standing still most of the day. I need to stretch my muscles."

"Sure," Darby easily agreed. She'd sleep even better if she got some exercise.

Early in the summer, she'd tethered a floating dock half a mile out in the lake for guests to use. Floodlights from the yard would illuminate their way, and it was a full moon tonight, which would give them even more light.

"Three miles?" she asked.

"That'll do it," Marta agreed. "Then wine. We get to celebrate this."

"Celebrate what? Not quite getting enough signatures?"

"Celebrate still having a chance, even though we experienced a setback."

"You're a true optimist."

"I find it helps."

As they'd done several times in the past, they decided to push a small dinghy out to the floater. The dinghy was stocked with towels, the wine, warm-up clothes and life jackets. It was also a means for them to paddle back to shore without getting wet again.

After swimming several laps, they pulled up onto the floater and changed out of the suits into sweatpants and jackets, rubbing their hair dry before opening the bottle of wine.

"This is paradise," Marta observed, settling onto one of the towels.

The moon was high in the sky, surrounded by pinpricks of stars. A soft breeze wafted the scent of pine from the hillsides, and the lake water lapped softly against the floater, little more than ripples on the calm surface.

"Can you imagine a freight train chugging past, spewing out diesel smoke and shaking the ground?" Darby pointed to a rise behind the Sierra Hotel building. It would travel the length of the lowest ridge, crossing Wren Road, where it would have to blow its whistle. They'd have to put a bridge across the creek, and the reverberation would carry across the lake for miles.

"What was it like?" Marta asked as she poured herself a glass of wine. "Being in a war zone?"

"I was mostly behind the wire," said Darby, taking the bottle from Marta and pouring her own glass. She didn't mind talking about her time overseas. She knew Marta wanted to understand her passion for keeping Sierra Hotel open.

She took a sip of her wine. "It's the uncertainty that gets to you. No matter how calm things might feel in the moment, at any second all hell can break loose."

"That's the problem with the trains." Marta nodded.

"The women who stay here might have just been in a war zone, maybe even a military firefight, or maybe they've chased gang members down the streets of Chicago. I can't imagine telling them that all will be calm and quiet, well, except for the sudden blasts and clattering from the freight trains. Can you imagine having that wake you up in the middle of the night? They'd be lunging for their firearms. They need a complete break," Darby ended. "A *complete* break from the stress."

Marta held up her glass in a mock toast. "Here's to defeating the mayor."

Darby saluted in return, wondering just how difficult that was going to be. "How long have you known him?" she asked.

"All my life. I used to have a crush on his brother, Travis. Most of the girls in my age group had a crush on one or the other. Or on Caleb Terrell, at least until he moved away."

"I can see it," Darby allowed. She'd seen both Travis Jacobs and Caleb Terrell around over the past three years.

"Forgetting for a second that Travis and Caleb are both married," Marta continued. "Which one do you find attractive?"

"Of the two of them?" It seemed like an odd, theoretical question.

"Of the *three* of them," Marta clarified.

"You're asking if I'm attracted to Seth?"

Marta grinned. "I'm trying to figure out your type."

"Seth's more my type than the other two." Darby didn't see much point in denying it. She'd trusted Marta with her secrets for a long time now. "I mean, they're all good-looking, but I guess I like the take-charge type, smart, committed, take-no-prisoners." She gave a little self-deprecating laugh. "Even if those prisoners are me."

Then she paused. "You know it occurs to me that I might not find him quite as sexy if he backed down. Do you suppose that's a terrible character flaw?"

"You find him sexy?"

Darby rubbed a fingertip along the rim of her wineglass. "I'm afraid I do."

Marta looked calculating again.

"What?" Darby prompted.

"I'm wondering if we can use that to help our cause. Any chance he reciprocates?"

"He was a little flirty the night of the barn raising. And again at the fair, there might have been a little something. But I have a feeling that was more of an automatic response to the fact that I'm female. I bet he flirts with everyone."

"I don't think so," Marta countered. "I've seen him with lots of women. He's quite circumspect."

"Hmmm." Darby let her mind go back over the memory. She knew she shouldn't care whether or not he found her attractive, but her ego kind of liked the idea.

"It's another option. Maybe you could flirt your way to a referendum."

"I think you're being ridiculously optimistic. But I have to admit, I did think about it."

"It couldn't hurt to try," Marta reasoned. "If the petition fails, maybe you could cloud his judgment with lust."

"Would you ever try something like that?" It didn't seem particularly noble, but Darby had no doubt it would work for some women.

"Sure," said Marta. "Depending on the circumstances, if the stakes were high enough."

"How high?"

"If somebody's life was on the line. Or if a thousand lives were on the line. How could you live with yourself if you didn't?" She grimaced.

"Alas, in this case, no lives are on the line."

"Disappointed?" Marta grinned.

"No." Darby emphatically shook her head. Well, maybe a little. If somebody's life were on the line, she'd have a perfectly noble excuse to flirt with Seth.

"Plus, you'd probably have to sleep with him to really make it work."

"Excuse me?" Darby's fantasy didn't extend that far. Well, not really.

"I don't think you've got that in you."

"Why not?" Darby demanded, before she realized how that would sound out loud.

Marta laughed at her.

"I mean, of course I don't." Darby shifted to her stomach, settling more comfortably on her towel. The prone position kept her below the freshening breeze.

"Though," Marta mused, leaning back on her elbows. "I suppose you could sleep with him recreationally. Do it for fun, and if it helps, it helps."

"That's ridiculous," Darby told both of them.

"I prefer to think of it as practical."

"Please tell me you're joking."

"I am, but not really. If, and only if, you'd be willing to sleep with him, anyway, why not let the chips fall where they may?"

Darby tried to picture it. Unfortunately, she could.

Three

Darby's petition was printed, bound and sitting on the breakfast table in the mayor's residence. Seth gazed at it while he sipped his orange juice and wondered about his next move. Some of the names he'd expected, others had surprised him, leading him to make some mental estimates about his chances in a full-on referendum. Would Darby be able to hold this level of support through a secret ballot? Or had they simply signed the petition to make a pretty woman happy?

Lisa appeared in her usual black slacks and dark blazer. She crossed the kitchen to the breakfast nook. There, she took a seat in the streaming sunshine, pouring herself a cup of coffee from the stainless vacuum pot.

"I have good news and bad news," she opened.

"I'm staring at the bad news already," Seth said.

"This is ironic," said Lisa.

"How so?"

She pointed to the petition. "*That's* the good news."

"I love it when you play mind games in the morning." It

took Seth an hour or so for his brain to be firing on all cylinders. But Lisa could hit the mental ground running.

"They don't have enough signatures."

Seth sat up straight, shaking some oxygen into his brain cells to make sure he'd heard right. "What?"

"They have five hundred ninety-seven signatures. We've double-checked."

Seth reached for the printout. "They actually lied?"

Darby was gutsier than he'd given her credit for. He found himself chuckling. After her accusing him of cheating, he couldn't wait to toss this in her face.

"They don't have the numbers." Lisa took a satisfied sip of her steaming coffee.

"So that's it." Seth's mood brightened considerably. "We're good to go. We can implement the permits tomorrow."

Finally, *finally,* he was going to accomplish something significant in this job. The hard work, the late nights, the compromises of his family—it was all going to be worth it.

"Not so fast," said Lisa.

He held his optimism in check. "Why?"

"Mountain Railway called. Well, one of their lawyers called."

"Don't tell me they've changed their minds." He tried to keep the fatalistic tone from his voice.

Seth knew the deal wasn't nailed down until every single piece was in place, formally signed and witnessed. And the recent negative press had been worrying him. He was afraid it would scare off the railway.

"They haven't changed their minds. During their legal review, they found a problem in a land survey."

He shifted gears. Problems, he could solve. Well, most of them. At least in the long run. "What did they find?"

"There's a discrepancy between the survey filed on the property title, and the survey filed in the Lands Office. And, in the case of a discrepancy, the Lands Office copy trumps anything else."

Seth waited for the bad news.

"Darby Carroll's land doesn't sit next to the proposed railroad right-of-way like we thought. The right-of-way crosses her land."

Frustration washed over him. "You have got to be kidding."

Darby owned part of the right-of-way? Was the woman his curse?

"I wish I was."

"By how much?"

"Her land goes over the right-of-way and half a mile past."

"Half a mile?"

"All the way up to the cliffs."

"That's ridiculous." Seth pushed back his chair. He'd seen the maps a hundred times.

"That's record keeping in the 1890s."

Lisa seemed far calmer than Seth felt, and it occurred to him that she might have a plan.

"Okay. Fine. If that's what it is, that's what it is. What's our best path forward?"

"We can ask her to grant an easement."

Seth scoffed his disbelief.

"I admit, it's a long shot," Lisa allowed.

"It's a no shot," he corrected. "Darby would laugh us into the next county."

"As mayor, you can expropriate," Lisa offered.

He was definitely willing to do that. After all, the woman had lied on her petition. As far as he was concerned, the gloves were off.

"How long will it take to expropriate?"

"If she draws it out?"

Seth set aside his napkin and came to his feet. "Oh, I think we can count on her drawing it out."

The gloves were coming off on both sides, and he'd be willing to bet she'd give him a run for his money.

"Days for sure," said Lisa. "Weeks, probably. It depends on the judge."

"Do we have any control over the judge?"

Lisa drew back, her brows shooting up. "You want to *influence the judge?*"

"No." Seth took a couple of paces across the kitchen. He hadn't realized how that could sound. "Of course I don't want to influence a judge. But I think it's fair game to get it in front of the right judge."

"Oh. Yeah. Maybe. If we time it right."

"By all means, let's time it right." He moved back to the table, swallowing the last of his coffee, figuring he was going to need the caffeine. "Any chance we can subtly slip through an easement request without her noticing?"

Lisa cocked her head. "You mean, hope she doesn't read the document before she signs it?"

"Good point. Okay, expropriation it is."

"The sooner we inform her, the sooner the formal process gets underway."

Seth picked up the petition. "I'll inform her myself. And while I'm at it, I think I'll ask her why she falsified a legal document."

He'd love it if there was a stiff penalty for having filed a bogus petition. If there was, he'd threaten to have her charged with the crime, then offer to let it go if she signed off on the easement.

He wanted to see her unnerved when she found out she was caught, watch her squirm, watch those big, green eyes widen with—

He stopped himself short.

What he really wanted to do was kiss her senseless. And that wasn't all he wanted to do to her. And his impulse had nothing whatsoever to do with any petition or railroad.

"Boss?" Lisa interrupted.

He shook himself. "What?"

"You faded away there for a minute."

"I'm plotting my strategy."

"Just don't make her mad," Lisa warned.

"She's already mad," he countered.

And then he was thinking about kissing her again, flattening her against a wall and pressing the length of his body against hers, delving into the sweetness of her mouth, making her pant and moan with—

Again, he pulled himself up short. "Cancel everything I have booked for today until you hear from me."

His number-one priority was Darby. No, that wasn't right. His number-one priority was the railroad. Darby was an obstacle to the railroad, and he had to get her out of the way.

Darby was halfway up a stepladder, rolling a coat of Summer Peach on the breakfast alcove wall, when a pounding threatened to cave in her front door. She'd been keeping herself busy all morning, trying to forget about the petition.

"Coming," she called out, wondering why whoever it was didn't just let themselves in. Her big foyer served as the lobby of the inn, and people were free to come and go.

She padded down the ladder, set the paint roller in the tray, wiped her hands on a rag and started for the great room.

The pounding came again.

"Come in," she called out this time, giving the furniture a wide berth in her paint-splattered clothes.

Nobody responded, so she gingerly turned the handle, pulling the door wide, coming face-to-face with Seth.

"Can I help you?" she asked, struggling to banish the guilt she was feeling from their petition subterfuge.

"I sincerely hope so," he answered, tapping a sheaf of papers against his palm.

It didn't take a rocket scientist to figure out what those papers were.

She kept her expression neutral, feigning innocence, inviting him to continue.

"There seems to be a small problem with your paperwork."

"Oh?"

"Oh?" he parroted, gaze hard and accusing.

"What's the problem?"

He cocked his head. "Are you really going to play innocent?"

"Innocent of what?"

He moved slightly closer. "You're a smart woman, Darby. And you know how to rise to a challenge. You don't have to cheat to get there."

She recognized her own words from their coffee at the Fall Festival. Okay, now she really felt guilty.

"Are you suggesting we miscounted?"

His eyes glittered with triumph. "Who said anything about the number of signatures being wrong?"

The question tripped her up, and it took her a moment to respond. "What else could it be?" she asked airily.

"About a dozen other things."

She could feel her face heat. "That seemed the most likely."

"At least you're a bad liar."

"What's that supposed to mean?"

"I mean, of all your many flaws, I don't have to add consummate liar to the list."

"What flaws?" she asked before she could catch herself. Why would she care if Seth thought she had flaws?

"You're caught, Darby. Own up to it."

"We may have miscounted," she admitted. "But that's hardly a crime."

"Punishable by a ten-thousand-dollar fine and up to three months in jail."

It took her a second to realize he was mocking her.

"Ha, ha."

He shrugged. "That's what it ought to be."

"You actually think I deserve jail?"

"It would keep you out of my hair."

"You just can't stand the fact that I'm right."

"You're not right."

She went for broke. "Then why does the idea of a petition scare you so much?"

"Do I look remotely frightened?"

She leaned her shoulder against the doorjamb. "If you weren't afraid of what I could do, you'd have sent somebody else up here to complain about the signature count."

"Wild speculation on your part." He braced his hand against the wall, close to her shoulder.

"Why are you here?"

"I don't need to send a minion to deal with you."

She wondered again about the plan to flirt with him. Was it crazy? Would it work? Would it put him off his game?

She seemed to be out of other options, so she tossed her hair back and let her gaze go soft. "Exactly how are you planning to deal with me, Seth?"

He blinked.

She added a coquettish smile for good measure.

He inched ever so slightly closer. "You really think that's going to work?"

"Do I think what's going to work?"

He leaned closer still. "You can't flirt your way out of the missing signatures. And what happened to you not flirting back?"

"Who's flirting back?"

He reached forward, resting his palm on her hip, his intense blue gaze trapping hers. "*You're* flirting."

"In your dreams, cowboy."

"Perhaps. But right now in real life, too."

The timbre of his voice made her chest tighten. Her pulse sped up, and a warm flush made her skin tingle.

His tone dropped to a lower rumble. "How far you going to take this?"

Excellent question.

While she struggled to come up with a reasonable answer, he eased forward. She told herself to back off, but for some reason, she didn't move. She told herself this was a terrible idea, but still, she didn't move.

He whispered her name in obvious frustration, and then his hot lips came down on hers.

The searing power of his kiss zipped through her nervous system, bringing her entire body to instantaneous life. He wrapped his arm around her, pressing it against her back. The doorjamb dug into her shoulder but she barely felt it. Endorphins and who knew what else had formed a hormone-fueled cocktail that took over her senses. All she felt was Seth.

He didn't let up. His lips urged hers open, while his tongue teased, and hers answered in kind. Her nipples tightened, and heat flooded her body, making her pliant and malleable.

When his hands moved to her bottom, urging her against his hard body, she came to him willingly. Her arms snaked their way around his neck, and she tilted her head while he deepened their kiss. His fingers then splayed into her hair, and the friction from his hard chest made her nipples tingle with desire.

Color and light swirled through her brain. The world tipped beneath her, and her equilibrium was lost. If not for Seth's enveloping hug, she might have tumbled to the porch.

Her one small scrap of sanity was no match for the avalanche of passion flooding her body. She had a sudden urge to tear off their clothes and make love right there on the front porch.

He drew back, dragging in breaths, looking as dazed as she felt. "Another minute, and I'll be swearing it's six hundred names."

Another minute and Darby would be sporting a train engineer's hat.

He dropped his hands and stepped back. "This could get me into a lot of trouble at the office."

"I'm sorry—" She stopped, not sure exactly what she was sorry about.

He laughed. "For being a great flirt? I've got to hand it to you, Darby. I didn't think you'd go through with a kiss."

Still feeling slightly unsteady on her feet, she forced out a casual laugh. There was no way she'd let him know how he'd affected her. "I figured it was worth a shot."

His expression turned serious. "Take another shot, any old time you'd like."

"We're getting more signatures," she told him, ignoring the urge to kiss him again right here and now. "Marta's out there signing more people up."

"You can't do that. The deadline's passed."

"There's nothing in the policy that says all six hundred have to be present at the deadline."

"That's the whole point."

"Maybe," she allowed. "Maybe not. But if you don't approve the referendum, I'll have to meet you in court so we can let a judge decide."

"Fightin' words, Ms. Carroll."

"You have paint on your jacket, Mr. Mayor."

He followed her gaze to the finger-shaped smears of peach where she'd gripped his sleeves. He blew out a heavy sigh.

"You're a regular walking disaster."

She stifled a smile. "I'll pay for the dry-cleaning."

He shrugged. "Sadly, the jacket barely registers on my radar today. There's also a problem with your property survey on file at the Lands Office."

The sudden change in topic took her by surprise.

"What problem?" She scrambled to figure out his new angle.

"Mountain Railway's lawyers did some research—"

"Oh, no, you don't," she interrupted. "You are *not* going to mess around with my land—"

"I'm not messing around—"

"I don't care who you are, Seth Jacobs." She closed the space between them, tapping her index finger against his chest. "I will not be—"

"You own more land than you thought," Seth all but shouted over her, grasping her paint-smeared hand and dragging it away from him.

"Huh?"

"The mistake is bad for *me*. I'm not here to cheat. Not that you don't deserve someone who plays dirty."

While he spoke, Seth suspiciously checked his shirtfront. "There was a mistake made in the survey record back in 1893. It turns out your land goes across the rail right-of-way. That being the case, we'll be asking you for an easement." He stopped talking.

The breeze gusted up from the lake, while songbirds darted from tree to tree.

"Are you saying I own more land?" She struggled to wrap her head around the news.

"Yes. The Lands Office will redraft your plan to match the one on the official file," Seth said.

"So the train would come *across* my land?"

"If you grant an easement," he confirmed.

"I don't see that happening."

"Neither do I," he admitted. "So I'll expropriate your land."

"You can't do that." If it was her land, she should have a say.

"Yes," he told her firmly, "I can."

She believed him. "I'll fight you."

Their relationship was about to get more adversarial than ever.

"You can't fight me on this one. And a petition won't help."

"Do you enjoy being the bad guy?" asked Darby.

"I've never been the bad guy. And I'm the good guy now. It's what the people want, Darby. Accept it and move on."

"A referendum will tell you what the people want."

He shook his head and drew away, looking every inch in control. "The election already told me that."

"What happens if they succeed?" Travis asked Seth from the passenger seat of the mayor's official car.

"Succeed at what?" Seth asked, needing Travis to narrow the question down. Darby Carroll was uppermost on his mind, but as mayor, he was battling problems on a whole lot of fronts right now.

The two men were driving along the River Road on the way to a Rodeo Association dinner. Seth was at the wheel of his official vehicle, working hard at avoiding potholes.

"Succeed in getting the railway referendum."

"They didn't get enough signatures."

"It might not matter," said Travis. "Abigail read the bylaw, and Darby isn't wrong. There's nothing specifically stopping her from submitting additional signatures after the petition is filed."

"It's going in front of Judge Hawthorn."

"So?"

"So, he grew up in the Valley. Half his family is still in ranching."

Travis frowned. "You're not saying what I think you're saying."

"I'm saying Judge Hawthorn will give us a straight-up reading of the bylaw and the intent of the bylaw. He's not going to go looking for esoteric little loopholes to derail progress."

"He's honor bound to follow the law."

Seth splashed the car through a puddle, knowing he'd have to get it washed yet again. "Exactly. I'm counting on that."

Red and yellow leaves fluttered in bursts from the woods, ticking their way across the windshield. Seth rounded a corner and came to a rolling field where cattle dotted the golden wheatgrass. Snow was gathering on the high, distant peaks, and a chill blew down from the mountains.

He angled the car into the gravel parking lot of the association's clubhouse, sliding it between a powder-blue pickup and a steel-gray SUV.

"Anything I can do to help?" Travis asked as they exited the car.

"I'm the one who ran for office," Seth responded, knowing, for better or worse, he was getting what he'd signed up for, and it was his responsibility to deal with the problems.

"If you'll recall, I tried to talk you out of it."

"I recall," Seth admitted.

He and his younger brother had had many lively arguments about his plan to become mayor.

"Are you saying I was right?" Travis pressed.

"I'm saying we've hit a snag." A very beautiful, very compelling, very sexy little snag.

"What's up with that expression?" Travis asked.

"What expression?" Seth focused on schooling his features.

"You looked kind of sappy there for a minute."

"I'm not sappy. I'm nervous. I have to give a speech now."

Travis scoffed out a laugh. "Liar. You've never been afraid of a podium before."

"It's been a tough week." With no interest in explaining further, Seth left Travis behind and strode into the crowded room.

There, he immediately spotted Darby.

There were a couple hundred people in the clubhouse, but his attention seemed to zero in on her like a heat-seeking missile. He hadn't expected her to be here.

Bad enough she was haunting his dreams. Did she also have to stalk his reality? The rodeo people were hardly her usual crowd. They were the ranchers, the hard-liners, the ones who were most angry at her stance on the railroad. She'd never get their support on a referendum or anything else.

But there she was, standing boldly in the lion's den. She wore a short, steel-gray skirt and a soft, gray, sparkly sweater, with black tights and black ankle boots that had a distinctly Western flair. Her wavy, auburn hair, which cascaded past her shoulders, was tucked behind her ears to show off a pair of dangling black earrings.

"Looking sappy again," joked Travis from behind him.

Ignoring his brother, Seth kept walking, moving closer to her.

As he made his way across the room, she was approached by Joe Harry. Joe was a big, ambling cowboy who'd barely made it through high school. He could work all day and party all night, but he wasn't the sharpest nail in the toolbox, and social niceties had never been his strong suit.

He was clearly agitated, towering above Darby, face contorted, gesticulating as he spoke. Her expression became pinched under the onslaught, and Seth quickened his pace.

"...don't know where the hell you get off," Joe was saying, "messing around with the things in this Valley. My family has lived here for a hundred years."

"As has mine," she returned. "My aunt—"

"But not you, missy." Joe waggled a finger in her face. "You're as new and—"

"Hello, Joe." Seth clapped the man firmly on the shoulder and held out his hand to shake. "I hear you gave Reed Terrell a run for his money in steer wrestling this year."

The interruption seemed to rattle Joe. It took a moment, but then he put out his hand to shake Seth's.

"Came second in overall points," he confirmed.

"Way to go," Seth said heartily. "That's impressive."

He gave Darby a fleeting glance. "Sorry to interrupt here, but I need to have a word with Darby."

Joe frowned. "I was in the middle—"

"Don't you worry about it," Seth said, leaning in and lowering his voice to an overtly conspiratorial level. "I've got this one covered."

"I've got some things to say to that woman."

"I understand your perspective." Seth nodded, his expression showing Joe he was taking this seriously. "And I do agree with you. My office is working on it."

Joe gave Darby a disparaging look. "It ain't right. She ain't right."

"I'm working to make it right," said Seth. "Why don't you

go on over to the bar." Seth fished into his pocket for the free drink tickets that had come with his invitation for the dinner. He handed Joe a red one. "Have a beer on me."

"That's kind of you, Mayor."

"Enjoy the evening." Seth turned from Joe to find Darby walking away.

"Hey." He stepped fast to catch up with her, touching her arm.

"What the hell was that all about?" She shook off his hand.

Seth was taken aback by her tone. "Joe was obviously bothering you."

"So you thought you'd *rescue* me?"

Seth's brain scrambled to make sense of her words. He hadn't expected outright gratitude, but he *had* done her a favor here.

"You'd rather I hadn't?" he asked.

"One kiss does not make me yours to rescue. And I'd rather you gave me a little credit. I can handle a guy like Joe Harry."

"I didn't rescue you because I kissed you."

"You don't get to rescue me for any reason at all."

"What's wrong?" he demanded.

"The usual."

She'd lost him. "What usual?"

"We're adversaries."

"That doesn't mean I'm not a gentleman."

"Forgive me if I doubt that declaration," she barely muttered. "Given your past behavior."

He didn't need to be a genius to guess what she meant. He moved in to keep his voice low. "You wanted that kiss as much as I did."

"I wasn't talking about the kiss. Besides, I was faking that."

Seth drew in a frustrated breath, telling himself to regroup. If she was faking it, that was an award-worthy performance. But now was definitely not the time to dwell on the sincerity of her kisses.

"I was trying to stop Joe from making a scene," he told her instead.

"I had it under control."

"You think?"

"I think."

"And what would you have done if he'd gotten out of hand?"

"Elbow him in the solar plexus. Break his nose with the heel of my hand. Knee him in the groin."

Seth couldn't help but wince at the last threat.

"Same things I'll do to you if you get out of hand."

"Then I'll be very careful not to get out of hand."

"Really?" She blinked at him. "When were you planning to start?"

Seth wished Darby would stop making him smile at such inappropriate times. The woman was threatening to emasculate him, but he couldn't help appreciating her quick retorts.

"You've taken self-defense classes?" he asked, trying to keep his amusement under wraps.

"I have."

"Where?" He wondered if they were offered locally. He hadn't heard about them.

"The United States Military."

"Excuse me?"

"You heard me. I'm a soldier. I remain a captain in the army reserve."

"A captain?"

That explained why she struck him as being so fit, so alert, so incredibly healthy. He couldn't help but be impressed.

"Yes," she answered.

"Were you overseas?"

She nodded. "I was."

"Where?"

"Don't you have to give a speech?"

"You've got me curious." What else didn't he know about her?

"Well, you're going to have to stay curious."

"I guess you could also shoot me?" he ventured with a grin.

"And I know how to lob a grenade." This time, it was Darby who was obviously fighting a grin.

"You don't have any of them on you, though. Grenades, I mean."

"Not tonight."

"Good to hear." Seth fought a strange feeling of warmth growing inside him.

He knew they were adversaries. He knew he shouldn't be attracted to her, and he sure shouldn't be flirting with her. Not that talking about grenades would normally be considered flirting. But some kind of energy sparked between them every time they had a conversation. And that spark made him want to keep the conversation going, to get her alone, to take her in his arms and kiss her all over again.

He knew his reaction was reckless and unprofessional, but it was also impossible to fight.

Four

Despite her own best intentions, Darby found herself engaging with Seth's speech. On stage in front of the Rodeo Association, he was keeping the two-hundred-odd members of the audience entertained and laughing with his anecdotes of previous rodeos. She hated to admit it, but she could definitely see how he'd been elected. He had an almost electric presence in front of a crowd, while keeping his stories down to earth in a way that obviously spoke to the cowboys in the audience.

The crowd was friendly to the railway, and when he closed with a plug for it, they erupted in enthusiastic applause.

With dinner over, she said goodbye to the other occupants at her table. They'd been polite but cool throughout the evening. There was no need for her to guess they were on Seth's side of the railway debate. Most people in Lyndon now knew who she was and what she was trying to accomplish.

When she turned from the table, she nearly walked into Seth.

"Heading home?" he asked, without backing off an inch.

"No. I'm going to stay and mingle," she responded. "Chat with the citizens."

Other people were rising from their chairs in the big hall, too, moving around to visit with each other. Darby's back was flush against her table, but a steady stream of guests passed behind Seth.

"You sure that's such a good idea?" he asked in the rising din of conversation.

"It's why I'm here."

His tone was serious. "The cowboys have been taking advantage of the bar, and you know you're a lightning rod."

She settled her small bag firmly on her shoulder, squaring them both to show she meant business. "I told you earlier. I can take care of myself."

"Fair enough. I'm just worried about the other guys."

"You're worried about your precious railroad."

"I don't want another Joe Harry incident."

"I'll avoid him."

"There are too many like Joe Harry for you to avoid them all. Why not wait until the judge rules on the referendum? You don't even know yet if we'll have one."

"Oh, you'd love a head start."

"If he doesn't rule in your favor, all of this, the stress, the risk—it will have been a waste of time."

"I'm not feeling any stress."

"Well, I sure am. Part of the mayor's job is to keep the peace."

"Don't worry about me, Seth."

"I do worry about you. And not just that you might get a referendum."

"I will get a referendum," she corrected him. "I'm an unstoppable force."

"And I'm an immovable object."

"Get out of my way."

He took a step to one side. "I mean that metaphorically."

She flexed a satisfied grin. "Oh, how I wish everything in life was that easy."

"You're free to move about the reception."

"I was never asking your permission." She brushed past him.

She angled toward the patio, where the doors had been thrown wide to let in the fresh air.

It was easy to find people with an opinion on the railway. Most of them disagreed with her, some quite vehemently. But she told them all about the potential referendum, anyway, that the judge would rule in the next few days, and she invited them to review all the facts on her website.

Suddenly, a beefy, powerful arm slipped around her neck, trapping her. She automatically threw an elbow backward, connecting with his ribs. The man grunted in pain, but his grip only tightened and he dragged her backward and off balance.

"Joe!" she heard Seth shout, and there was a sound of boots hitting the floor at a run.

Darby elbowed her captor again, earning another grunt along with a shot of pain running up her arm. Joe lifted her all the way off the floor, and she was struggling to breathe. She kicked backward, but her heels skidded against the side of his legs. Without a visual, it was hard to land a direct hit.

Then Seth was there, wrenching Joe's arm. Seth's brother, Travis, grabbed Joe from the other side.

"Let her go!" Seth demanded, sheer violence in his tone as he yanked on the big man's arm. "Right now, Joe. Right *now*."

The pressure eased on Darby's neck, telling her Seth was succeeding. But Joe didn't let her go completely, and she was still pressed against his body.

"Phone the sheriff," Travis shouted.

"Darby?" Seth called. "Are you okay? Say something."

She tried to speak, but nothing came out. She was breathing, she told herself. She might have a bruise or two, but she wasn't in mortal danger. She elbowed and kicked one more time.

Joe suddenly let her go.

She staggered to the ground, nearly falling, catching herself just in time, blinking the world back into focus.

"You okay?" Seth called to her again.

She managed a nod. "Fine," she rasped, drawing rapid breaths.

"What is the *matter with you?*" Seth shouted at Joe, straightening his shoulders, causing Joe to take a step back.

The man didn't seem to have anything to say.

"I'll take him home," came another male voice from the crowd.

"Take him to the sheriff," Seth countered.

"He needs to sleep it off."

"He can sleep it off in jail. Travis, go with them."

Travis gave Seth a sharp nod. "You got it."

Seth immediately moved to Darby, his arm going around her shoulders. "You okay?"

"Good. Yeah, fine. Maybe some air." She could feel dozens of pairs of eyes on her. They didn't look particularly friendly, and the last thing she needed was to seem weak.

She straightened, shrugged off Seth's arm, managed a smile and made her way toward the big, open doors.

Seth followed.

"I'm fine," she told him with conviction as they walked.

"So you say."

"You can leave me alone now."

"I don't think so."

"Sure you can. Joe's on his way to jail, and everyone else has gone back to dancing."

"You've annoyed more than just Joe tonight. Who knows who else might be looking to get in on the action."

Darby wasn't afraid of anyone else. Joe's action was a one-off. Lyndon Valley was full of peaceful, law-abiding citizens. She made it to the doors and walked through. The cool breeze was welcome. She inhaled deeply, rubbing her neck where Joe had held her so tight.

"Do you need to see a doctor?" asked Seth.

"No." She was fine. Well, she would be fine, and soon.

"You sure?"

"I'm sure." She made her way down the length of the sun-deck, into the shadows where the bright stars provided the only illumination. She sat down on a narrow bench, craning her neck, when Seth stopped directly in front of her.

"You going to follow me around all night like some exasperating bodyguard?"

"I was thinking I'd take you home."

"I can drive. And I'm not ready to leave yet."

He sat down beside her, stretching out his legs. "Have it your way."

"Seth?" came a woman's voice.

Abigail Rainer, formerly Abigail Jacobs, and one of Seth's sisters, had followed them out to the wooden deck. Abigail was quite obviously pregnant, and Darby had been hoping to leverage the woman's maternal instincts to make her question the wisdom of the railway.

"Hey, Abby," Seth responded, rising to his feet.

"Hello." Darby rose with him.

"You must be Darby Carroll," Abigail said.

"I am."

"Are you all right?"

"I'm perfectly fine. I'm sorry to have caused such a scene."

"It's not your fault. Joe never was the most reasonable of men. As long as you're not hurt."

"I offered her medical attention," Seth noted.

"Why don't you head on inside," Abigail suggested to Seth. "I was hoping Darby and I would have a chance to talk."

"You were?" Darby couldn't quite hide the surprise in her tone.

"Run along, Seth," Abigail directed.

"Yes, do run along, Seth," Darby echoed, not quite hiding the thread of amusement in her voice. She'd never have thought of Abigail as an ally.

Seth looked from one woman to the other. He hesitated, but then marched away, grumbling under his breath.

Abigail perched herself on the bench, and Darby followed suit.

"So, I heard you were giving my brother a run for his money."

"I'm trying." Darby couldn't help but be puzzled by Abigail's friendliness.

"Good," Abigail chirped.

"Good?"

"I like to hear all sides of an issue." Abigail gave an airy shrug. "I particularly like to talk to smart people who disagree with me. You strike me as a smart person who will undoubtedly disagree with me."

Darby wasn't sure if she should be flattered or not. At the same time, she couldn't help but contrast Abigail's equanimity with Seth's obstinacy.

Abigail gave a disarming grin. "It helps me understand things better."

"In that case, I'm more than happy to assist. What would you like to disagree with me on?"

"How long have you lived in the Valley?"

"Three years," said Darby. "I inherited the place near Berlynn Lake from my great-aunt."

"Mona Reese."

"You knew her?"

"I met her a few times. She had a reputation for being independent and no-nonsense."

"I only met her a few times, myself," Darby admitted.

"Really?" Abigail's tone invited more information.

"We weren't a large family, or a close family. It was just my mom and me growing up."

Abigail's expression was sympathetic.

"I guess that's hard for you to imagine," said Darby, for some reason feeling slightly embarrassed.

"Well, the Jacobs clan has always been close and big." Abigail's hand went to her stomach. "Getting bigger all the time."

Darby took the opening. "When is your baby due?"

"January. Four more months."

"You look really good." For a woman who was five months pregnant, Abigail looked extraordinarily fit and healthy.

"I feel a little tired," she admitted.

"Do you know if it's a boy or a girl?"

"A boy," said Abigail. "A cousin for Asher to play with."

"Asher's your nephew?" Darby had researched the whole Jacobs family, but she wanted to keep the conversation going in this direction.

"My sister Mandy's son. It might sound sexist, but boys are always good news for a ranching family."

"I thought you lived at the DFB Brewery now."

"I do." Abigail nodded. "But I'll always have roots at the ranch. But you want to talk about the train."

"Yes, I would like that." Darby nodded. "I can't help wondering if the price we'd pay as a community would be worth the monetary savings from moving cattle."

"What do you think we'd give up?"

"Peace," Darby said. "Quiet. I know DFB is becoming a popular tourist stop."

"Trains would bring more tourists," Abigail countered.

"There are plans for passenger service?" Darby hadn't heard anything about passenger service.

"Not immediately, but you never know, once the tracks are in place…"

"You don't think your customers would rather have the quiet ambiance and drive to DFB?"

"I truly don't know."

Darby decided to try another tactic. "You grew up in Lyndon Valley, right?"

"I did."

"Did you like it?" Darby glanced at Abigail's swollen belly.

"Would you like your own children to grow up in the same kind of Lyndon Valley that you enjoyed as a child?"

"I don't agree that a train would so fundamentally change the character of the Valley. Though I do believe that's your strongest argument."

Darby thought it was, too, though she was surprised to hear Abigail say so. "Do you worry about safety?"

"There's already a lot of danger on a ranch," said Abigail. "Kids need to learn how to avoid it from a young age."

Darby hadn't thought of it from that perspective. She supposed train crossings were no more perilous than angry bulls.

Abigail leaned forward. Her expression and tone were still open and friendly. "Can I ask you a question?"

"Of course."

"What's really going on here, Darby? You seem more passionate about this than makes sense."

"I like Berlynn Lake the way it is," said Darby. "And my customers—all women, by the way—are looking for a respite."

"From?" asked Abigail.

"Very, very stressful lives." Darby wished she could elaborate. It might gain her some sympathy. But she needed to keep Sierra Hotel's clientele a secret. If it became general knowledge that military strategists, covert operatives and criminal gang specialists frequented her inn, a whole host of enemies could take an interest in the place.

"The rail will cross right through my property," she continued. "Hundred-car freight trains will shake the ground, and the whistles will bounce across the lake day and night."

"I haven't been up there in years."

"You should come up," Darby said. "And remind yourself how beautiful it is." She couldn't help smiling. "You might want to make it soon. Since you'll probably get really busy in the next few months."

Abigail returned the smile. Then she rose to her feet. "Maybe I will."

Darby stood with her.

"But for now," said Abigail, "I'm going to find Sawyer. This mommy-to-be needs her sleep."

"Thank you for listening," said Darby.

"It was good to meet you. You're not nearly as bad as Seth makes out."

"Seth's talked about me?" Darby didn't know why that surprised her. It made sense that Seth would complain about her to his family, probably to anyone else who would listen, as well.

"You get under his skin," said Abigail. She seemed to consider Darby.

"I wish he would listen to reason," Darby remarked.

"He's listening," said Abigail. "He's just disagreeing with you."

"Of course." Darby backed down. "I'm sorry. I didn't mean to insult—"

"It's fine, Darby. You're allowed to fight with my brother. It's probably good for him. Most of his successes in life have come way too easily."

Darby read between the lines. "You expect him to win."

"I expect him to win," Abigail confirmed. "But that doesn't mean you should stop trying."

"Oh, I'll keep trying," Darby said.

"There's Sawyer." Abigail nodded along the sundeck. "I'll call you if I can make it to Berlynn Lake."

"No need to call," said Darby. "Stop by anytime."

She watched while Abigail made her way toward her husband.

Darby watched as he smiled warmly at his wife, closing the distance between them, taking her arm, whispering something that made them both grin.

Darby couldn't help being slightly jealous of the romantic picture. Not that she sought a hearth, home and white picket fence. But having a man look at you like you were the only thing that mattered in the world was rather compelling.

As they disappeared, Seth returned, making his way back to Darby.

"How'd it go?" he asked. "Any luck co-opting my sister?"

"I think so. She seemed open to my arguments."

"You're lying." He sat down beside her, so close they were almost touching.

"Abigail has a mind of her own. She's not always going to toe your family line." Darby knew she should put some space between her and Seth, but for some reason she stayed put.

"She understands the importance of the railroad. She's a rancher."

"She's a brewery owner. And she's going to be a mother."

"Doesn't make her any less of a rancher."

Darby paused and studied him. "Interesting logic you've got going there."

"She grew up on a ranch and is every bit as much a shareholder in the family ranch corporation as I am."

"So, you're still a rancher?"

"Yes, ma'am."

"Then how can you represent the interests of the non-ranching community as mayor?"

"I concentrate really, really hard."

"Seth—"

"Darby, we can go round and round this all night long."

She couldn't disagree. "I suppose arguing with each other is pointless." It wasn't like either of them was going to budge.

"It is pointless. You want to talk about something else? Maybe something we can agree on?"

"You can think of something we'd agree on?"

"Not off the top of my head. You?"

"I like apple pie," she offered, deciding she needed a mental break from sparring with Seth.

He smiled at that.

"I like baseball," he returned.

"Motherhood," said Darby.

"Where do you stand on ice cream?"

"Butter pecan?"

"My favorite," said Seth.

"Who'd have thought?"

"Kisses?" he asked, his voice a low, sexy rumble.

"Excuse me?" She pretended not to have heard properly, but her heart gave a deep, hard thump.

He eased slightly closer, his thigh touching against hers. "Kisses from one particular woman."

Darby's throat went dry. This was not a good direction. Not at all.

She rose to her feet, intending to leave, but he caught her hands.

"I thought kisses might be something we could agree on."

"We can't go there," she breathed.

His hands were warm—no, hot—and the way they held hers was a perfect blend of strength and tenderness. Arousal once more percolated its way through her body, sensitizing her skin.

"We're already there." His tone was deep and compelling.

"Seth," she protested.

"We should do it again."

"Here?" she asked incredulously, glancing around. "Now?"

"Or later." His gaze was intense. "In the mayor's residence."

Desire flashed through her, along with an excruciatingly detailed memory of being held in his arms. "You know I can't say yes to that."

"I know you won't."

"We're locked in a battle."

"I thought we were trying to mitigate it."

"By *sleeping together?*"

His mouth quirked in a quick grin. "I said kissing."

"You meant sex." Of that, she was completely certain.

"I wouldn't say no to sex." He reeled her slightly closer.

She could have pulled back, but she didn't. "That's because you're a man."

"Are you calling me easy?"

She was standing almost between his thighs, the heat of them swirling out, permeating her thin, black tights. "I'm calling your entire gender easy."

He reached up and put his hand to the back of her neck. "No problem. We can take the hit."

"What are you doing?" she breathed.

He urged her face toward his. "You said no to later, so I'm going with now."

"You're going to kiss me?"

"That's the plan."

"Why?"

"Because you're pretty," he rumbled. "Because you smell nice. Because you're soft and sexy."

"Are you trying to manipulate me?" she asked.

"Into kissing me?"

"Into changing my mind."

He raised a brow. "Are you trying to manipulate me into changing *my* mind?"

"Yes," she admitted, subconsciously easing toward him, inhaling his scent, her pulse speeding up, her skin beginning to tingle.

"Me, too." He stretched up to meet her. "Let's see who wins."

His kiss was even better than she remembered. His lips were firm and hot. He reached up to cradle her face with his hands, thumbs stroking her cheeks, fingers splaying into her hair.

Her knees quickly grew weak, and she sank down onto his knee, wrapping her arms fully around his neck, once again molding her body against his. His tongue teased hers, and she responded with a shiver, her skin rippling in goose bumps that went hot, then cold, then hot again.

Desire gathered in the base of her belly, flaring insistently downward. She squirmed against his thigh, her mouth opening wider to the heat of his kiss. His palms slid along her sides, skimming her breasts, following the curve of her waist to settle on her hips. He pressed her against him, and she moaned.

"Who's winning?" he rasped.

Through the electrified jumble of her brain cells, she struggled to form a sentence. "I don't think it's me," she told him honestly.

"I think it's you." He kissed her again, strong arms wrapping around her waist. "Because it sure isn't me."

Then he stood, drawing her to her feet, pressing his body flush against hers. He stroked her hair, and his voice was guttural in her ear. "Later? At the mayor's mansion?"

Her mind went to war with itself.

She couldn't sleep with him. She had to stay sharp. She had to keep her emotions out of the equation. If the citizens of Lyndon even suspected she had the hots for the mayor, it would fundamentally undermine her position.

Or could she? If they kept it secret? If they didn't tell a living soul, not even Marta?

"I take it that's a no." He eased back to gaze at her.

"It's a yes," she told him impulsively. If it wasn't for everything going on around them, she'd have easily agreed to meet him later. She could do this guilt-free.

He searched her expression, clearly astonished.

As the silence stretched, she told herself to hold her ground, not to lose her nerve.

He eased slightly farther away. "You're messing with my head."

She wasn't.

He shook his head. "You're manipulating me. There's no way you're showing up at my house."

Her first instinct was to correct him.

But thankfully, good sense returned before she could open her mouth. What was she thinking? She couldn't meet Seth at his house for a clandestine fling. It was the craziest idea she'd ever had.

She stepped fully away from him, smoothing out both her clothes and her expression. "What was your first clue?"

Seth had suspected from the beginning that Darby had the power to mess with his mind. But even his worst fears hadn't come close to reality. He couldn't forget about her, couldn't concentrate on work.

It didn't help that Judge Hawthorn had accepted the petition to hold a referendum. In a long speech, saying he was acting in the best interests of civic order and for the good of Lyndon City, he ruled in Darby's favor, granting the referendum.

By Friday afternoon, Seth realized he had to take a break from the fray. He'd left the office early and driven the two hours to his family's ranch, intending to put some miles between him and Darby, clear his head and put together a plan for fighting the referendum.

Back at home, things were comfortable, logical and predictable. The fields were still green and lush. Herefords dotted the Valley and the hillsides amongst the red and orange maple groves, the Rockies rising up, white-peaked in the distance, while the wide Lyndon River flowed endlessly through the middle of the spread. Barns, outbuildings and corrals stretched out to the north. A horse whinnied in one of the pens, snorting its curiosity at his arrival.

He got out of the pickup, his cowboy boots puffing the dust at the edge of the driveway turnaround. His brother, Travis, was the only Jacobs still living full-time in the two-story house that overlooked the river.

"Prodigal son," he heard Travis say from an open barn door.

"I've only been away two weeks," Seth pointed out, crossing the driveway to meet his brother. "And you were in Lyndon with me half the time."

Travis stripped off a worn leather glove and shook Seth's hand.

"How are things going here?" Seth asked.

Travis was number two in the Jacobs birth order. Seth was the oldest. After Travis came their sister Abigail, then Mandy and finally their baby sister Katrina, who'd left Lyndon Valley years ago to go to boarding school and become a ballerina. She'd only come back last year when she fell in love with their neighbor, Reed Terrell.

"Same old, same old," Travis replied, lifting his Stetson then replacing it on his head at a different angle. "Everybody's out on the range, rounding 'em up. I just replaced a couple of shoes. You here to work?"

"Taking a break from the fray," Seth admitted. "But I could work while I'm doin' it."

Travis grinned. "You thirsty?"

"Yeah," said Seth, turning toward the house. "Got any of Dad's Glen Klavit?"

"That kind of thirsty?"

"That kind of getting away from the fray. Judge Hawthorn threw a wrench into the works. And the good citizens of Lyndon are making me nuts." Seth didn't bother mentioning that it was one particular Lyndon citizen who was threatening to push him over the edge.

"I heard about the ruling. You think she'll win?"

"A lot of people want that railroad." Seth couldn't imagine them voting it down. "But I have to fight her, and that's going to take a lot of energy away from other things."

Travis slapped him on the shoulder. "On the bright side, you're not likely to get physically injured fighting Darby Carroll, where I just got kicked in the shoulder by an ornery mare."

"Cowboy up," Seth automatically responded.

"She called here," Travis added unexpectedly.

Seth stopped and turned. "Darby called here?"

"She did, indeed. Wanted to thank me for helping out with Joe, and then went on about the referendum, of course. She seems quite fearless."

Seth would have liked to ask what she'd said, but the whole point of coming out here was to forget about Darby.

"I particularly don't want to talk about her." He hooked his Stetson on a peg inside the door and ambled his way into the living room. He glanced at his watch, noting it was nearly seven. "You got anything to throw on the barbecue?"

"You don't want to talk about her?"

"That's what I said."

"Why not?"

Seth turned to face his brother. "Wouldn't explaining the reason be, in fact, talking about her?"

Travis's gaze took on a speculative gleam. "I saw the way you looked at her at the Association dinner. Something happen between the two of you?"

"Nothing happened."

"You want something to happen?"

"Can't a guy get a drink and a burger in peace around here?"

"Whoa." Travis held up his hands in mock surrender.

Then his cell phone rang, but he gave Seth a long, suspicious look before retrieving it from his pocket.

"Yeah?" he answered.

His expression stilled. "Where?"

Seth felt his senses go on alert.

"We'll mount up. Right now." Travis stuffed his phone back into his pocket and turned for the front door.

Seth swiftly fell into step. "What's going on?"

"Stampede coming up on Barrel Ridge. There's only two cowboys on the herd, and they don't think they can turn it."

"Headed this way?" asked Seth, grabbing his hat and setting his brain on the potential for damage and injury.

They jogged down the front stairs. Travis beelined for the barn, while Seth rang the brass bell hanging on the porch to alert hands and their families. Hearing the signal, any available cowboys would rendezvous at the barn, while mothers would get their children into the nearest building.

Things went wrong on a cattle ranch, and people had to react quickly. It might be a rogue bull, a grass fire or a stampede. There'd be time enough for explanations later. For now, people just needed to get out of the way.

Seth loped across the driveway into the barn, stopped at the tack room to load up then headed straight for the stall of Yellowtail, one of the fastest, steadiest horses on the ranch.

Travis was saddling up Nomad, a six-year-old he'd trained from birth while two other cowboys, Frank Stone and Nevada Williams, scrambled to get their own mounts ready.

"North around the pond?" Travis shouted to Seth.

"Seems like the best plan," Seth agreed, settling the bit. "I'll take point if you can clean it up."

Travis nodded. "Stone, ride with me. Nevada, try to stay on Seth's heels."

"Got it, boss," Nevada swung into his saddle.

Seth tucked in the cinch strap and mounted up.

The four men left the barn on a gallop. Seth was relieved to see the yard deserted. If they couldn't turn the herd, bedlam was going to strike here in about ten minutes.

Seth crouched low, while Yellowtail stretched into a full gallop. She was a big, long-legged mare, and she liked nothing better than having a job to do. She easily outpaced the other three horses, smoothing out the uneven ground, responsive to Seth's lightest cues.

He crested the first hill and saw the stampeding herd in the distance. Their path was exactly as he'd expected, and he gave an arm signal to the others, telling them to go around the pond. They'd come up on the east side of the herd, turning them west, circling them back, letting them run off any lingering steam in the open meadow.

Yellowtail's ears pricked up. She knew the drill. Seth guided her past the pond, down a short trail through an aspen grove, then out to the wheatgrass hillside. He watched the lead cattle, studying their body language, letting Yellowtail navigate the way down the slope.

It was suicide to get in front of the cattle, so he brought his horse alongside, checking quickly over his shoulder to make sure Travis and the others were close enough for backup.

He gave a shout, easing Yellowtail into the flank of an outside cow. It shifted its path, nudging the one next. Seth narrowed the gap, shouting, waving his hat, closing down the pathway.

He heard Nevada call out behind him, making sure the next wave of cattle started to turn. The minutes seemed like an eternity of thundering hooves and choking dust. He would have given pretty much anything for a kerchief to cover his mouth and nose.

He spat out the gritty taste, lowering his hat to protect his eyes. A heifer sprang out, but Yellowtail was on her in a flash. Seth quickly rebalanced in his saddle as they chased the animal back to the main herd.

The turn was working. The animals' pace was slowing. Through the waves of dust, he could see Travis and Stone far across the herd, and the original two cowboys completing the circle. The cattle started to bawl, moving to a walk, settling down.

Nevada moved up beside him. "That'll get your adrenaline flowing."

"Been a while since I've done that," Seth noted, swiping an arm across his sweaty forehead.

"Good to see the city hasn't made you soft."

Seth laughed. "Bein' the mayor is a lot like bein' a cowboy. Difference is, herding voters is more like herding cats. At least the Herefords are predictable."

Travis whistled, and Seth glanced up.

"Might as well pen 'em up," Travis shouted.

Seth waved his agreement, and he and Nevada took up positions, moving the cattle the last couple miles to one of the home fields, where the herd could graze for the next few weeks before the final roundup.

It was nearly ten by the time Seth and Travis made it back

to the ranch house. They were both in need of a shower, but instead they stretched out on the deck chairs of the veranda, each twisting the cap off a bottle of beer.

"Welcome home," said Travis, raising his bottle.

"I've missed it," said Seth, taking a drink and letting the cool liquid soothe his dry throat.

"Not enough excitement for you up there in the big house?"

"I like the logic and simplicity here," Seth explained. "Roundup good. Stampede bad. Mission, stop stampede. And now the stampede is stopped, and we can relax."

Travis laughed, lifting one booted foot to rest it on the bench seat of a picnic table. "That's not how it works in politics?"

"In politics, the cattle would be clustered in a secret corner of the field, plotting how to take down the fence, hijack the transport truck and firebomb the barn. While the horses would have unionized by now and demanded more oats."

"You clearly have a burr in your butt."

"I clearly do."

"Darby Carroll?" Travis asked.

Seth glared at him.

"Hey, you flat-out refuse to talk about something, I gotta figure it's the one thing that's bugging you the most."

"You're starting to sound like our sisters."

"What?" Travis scoffed. "You think I care about your feelings? I just want to harass you."

Seth took another drink, gazing at the distant mountains, black against the rising moon.

"She's smart," he said into the silence. "She's committed and hardworking. And she kisses like there's no tomorrow."

"You've been kissing your archenemy?"

"I have," Seth admitted.

"Go, big brother."

Seth chuckled. Then he sobered. "I just needed to get away from it all."

"'It all' being Darby?"

"'It all' being the complications and machinations of the mayor's office. To top it off, the governor's office left me a message this morning."

"The governor of Colorado?"

"Uh-huh."

"Why?"

"I haven't called him back yet. I'm guessing the president of Mountain Railway called him, expressing concern about the situation."

"'The situation' being Darby Carroll's crusade against the railroad."

"That would be the one."

Travis contemplated while he took a swig of his beer. "You might want to stop kissing her."

"I might *have* to stop kissing her," Seth allowed. "I don't see myself *wanting* to stop."

Five

The summons from the governor's office took Darby by surprise. She was told the state had put together a commission to consider new state-wide regulations for rail expansion, and they wanted to hear from her. Marta offered to hold down the fort at Sierra Hotel so Darby could travel to Denver and, hopefully, inspire the state to intervene in the Lyndon Valley rail project. It was an unexpected development, but it could easily work in their favor. If the decision was taken out of the town's hands, they'd definitely have a better chance of success.

Optimistic, Darby got up at 3:00 a.m. to make a dawn flight out of Lyndon to Denver. Though she got stuck in a middle seat between two large men and in front of a crying baby, she polished her presentation on the way.

She didn't have time for breakfast after landing. She was too nervous, anyway. Instead, she rushed to the state capitol building, determined to be on time and impress the members of the committee.

Shown to a waiting room, she was surprised to find Seth

already there. He looked crisp and fresh in a well-cut suit and a pressed white shirt. His burgundy-and-navy tie was precisely knotted. His face was shaved close. And his hair was perfectly trimmed.

"Good morning, Darby," he offered, not seeming at all surprised to see her.

"Good morning," she returned, attempting to hide her own surprise.

She hadn't counted on rebutting his arguments. Then again, she'd done it before. At least with Seth, she knew what to expect. Still, it was hard not to feel outclassed by his professional appearance. He must have flown in last night and stayed at a hotel.

She took a seat in a chair in the small room. "You're presenting, too?"

"I am."

"That's too bad."

"You hoped to have the floor all to yourself?"

She pulled a comb out of her purse, ran it through her hair and refastened her ponytail. "I did."

"Sorry to disappoint you."

"Not your fault. I should have guessed they'd want both sides, and you are a natural choice."

"The governor does like to keep things fair."

"I'll definitely be counting on that." Trying to keep her confidence at a peak, she smoothed the wrinkles out of her navy skirt and checked her white blouse beneath the matching navy blazer.

"You'll do fine, Darby," Seth told her kindly.

In return, she put as much condescension into her voice as she could muster. "I'm sure you will, too, Seth."

A woman appeared through a set of oversize double doors. "Mayor Jacobs? Ms. Carroll? The commission is ready for you both."

Great. They were presenting together. Not that she was going to say anything he hadn't heard before. But she'd prefer not to have him frowning or smirking while she made her points.

The room was opulent and airy. Arching, white beams glimmered around them, and the domed ceiling was covered in a mural. In the center was a huge, U-shaped table, and their footsteps echoed on the marble floor as they approached.

There were about thirty people sitting around the table. To a person, they were sixtysomething men with gray hair or balding heads. All wore dark suits and tight neckties. Another dozen or so people sat on chairs around the edges of the room, mostly women, obviously support staff.

Darby didn't know why she was surprised at the continuing gender divide in politics. Here, as in the military, women needed to support each other.

She took one of the two vacant chairs at a long table in the hollow end of the U-shape. There was a microphone in front of her, a glass of water, a pen and a pad of paper. She placed her purse on the floor and opened up her leather folder full of handwritten notes from the plane, laying them out in front of her.

Beside her, Seth sat smoothly down. He didn't have a briefcase, nor did he produce any speaking notes. The Chair invited him to go first.

Speaking from memory, Seth's presentation was organized and sharp. It highlighted the economic interests of Lyndon Valley, his election platform, Mountain Railway's record across the country and the expected benefits of the railway to the region. As he had at the Rodeo Association dinner, he kept the members of the commission engaged and interested with anecdotes that illustrated his points.

Darby, by contrast, fumbled. Her facts and figures were all there, as was her rationale and passion. But she lacked Seth's eloquent, effective delivery style. And when it came time for questions, it was clear that the railroad supporters outnumbered detractors.

The hours dragged on, past the expected noon end time. As

the clock crept toward 2:00 p.m., Darby realized she wouldn't make her return flight.

One of the commission members, a portly, older man who clearly enjoyed the sound of his own voice, launched into a lengthy dissertation on his positive experiences with the railroad as a young man, using up an additional half hour. By the time the Chair brought the gavel down on the discussions, Darby was tired, hungry and disillusioned.

"Well, that was fun," Seth mumbled to her as the commission members gathered their belongings and the staffers rose from the perimeter chairs to talk to the members.

"I'd say you won that round," Darby conceded.

"I don't think anything will come of it," he returned easily.

"What do you mean?" She tucked her papers away, zipping the edges of the folder.

"They want bragging rights for having convened a commission and interviewed stakeholders. They don't want to actually go to the trouble of enacting any new regulations."

"You mean to say, this was a waste of our time?"

There was a rebuke in his tone. "Darby Carroll, participating in the democratic processes of your state is never a waste of your time."

"Yeah, yeah. Well, I sure wish I'd brought a change of underwear to this particular democratic process."

Seth chuckled as he stepped to one side, letting her precede him to the door. "You were that nervous?"

"What?" Then she realized what he meant. "Of course not." She frowned at his juvenile humor. "I meant I missed the last flight back to Lyndon."

She adjusted the strap of her purse on her shoulder, tucking the folder under her arm as she stepped through the open doorway. "I'll have to find a hotel and try to get the flight tomorrow. Did you stay somewhere nearby?"

"I flew into Denver this morning." He opened the waiting-room door for her, and they started down the hallway.

"I didn't see you on the plane."

There were only a few flights a day out of the tiny Lyndon airport. It was odd that she could have missed him.

"My brother-in-law Caleb was in town. He lent me his corporate jet."

Darby sighed in resignation of the way the world worked. "You flew in on a corporate jet, looking like a million bucks, to present to a jury of your clones. Must be nice."

"You think I look like a million bucks?"

"I had to get up at 3:00 a.m. And a baby cried behind me the whole flight. I took a packed shuttle bus from the airport, and there wasn't a single woman on the commission. Did you notice that?"

"I'm sorry," he said simply.

"It's not your fault," she grumbled, suddenly embarrassed by her bad mood. "It's the lack of sleep. And the shameless waste of my time. I have a new group of guests coming in today, and now Marta has to take care of them until tomorrow afternoon."

He pressed the elevator button. "Let me buy you dinner."

"I don't need you to babysit me." She was a grown woman. While it might be inconvenient, she was perfectly capable of taking care of herself for twenty-four hours in Denver.

"Okay, you buy me dinner."

"Why would I do that?"

The elevator pinged, and the doors slid open to reveal an empty car.

Seth put his arm out to keep the door from sliding closed, gesturing her inside. "I'll make you a deal. I'm starving. You buy me something to eat at the bistro across the street, and I'll give you a ride home."

Darby turned inside the elevator, hoping he meant what she thought he meant.

"You mean today? In your corporate jet?" That would make her life a whole lot easier.

He pressed the button for the lobby, and they began their descent.

"Today. In my corporate jet," he affirmed.

"Your brother-in-law won't mind you picking up hitch-hikers?"

"Of course he won't mind. The thing has a dozen seats. And you don't look like you weigh much." Seth made a show of eyeing her up and down. "I doubt we'll notice the increase in jet fuel consumption."

The doors slid open at the lobby level, and they entered a brightly lit atrium.

"In that case, I am definitely buying you dinner. Thank you, Seth," she told him sincerely.

If they weren't battling over such an important issue, she would have admired his manners and his class. She also would have admired his public-speaking skills and his over-all professionalism. He wasn't a jerk. He was simply wrong about this one very important issue.

"You don't have to buy me dinner," he said.

"Yes, I do. That was the deal."

"I was only joking. I'm a gentleman. I'll still buy."

She shook her head. "It's not a date. And I'm paying."

"Okay," he finally agreed as they exited to the sidewalk. "But one dinner doesn't mean I'll sleep with you."

"Imagine my disappointment," she returned, even as a glow of awareness came to life inside her.

"I should tell you I'm still joking." He paused, tone gruff. "I'd sleep with you if you bought me coffee."

The little glow became insistent inside her. She had to struggle to keep her expression neutral. "It would pretty much take a corporate jet to buy your way into my bed."

He arched a brow. "That would do it? Because I could probably get a decent price from Caleb."

She shot him an exaggerated look of disdain. "And you claim ranchers need a break on transportation costs."

He laughed at that.

The light changed, and they crossed four lanes of traffic, taking a short staircase down to the Tableau Bistro.

It was dark inside, intimate and mostly deserted, since it was barely past the middle of the afternoon. Yellow candles glowed on each of the heavy wood tables. They were surrounded by high-backed, burgundy upholstered chairs. Pot lighting illuminated rich wooden walls, and a row of ceiling arches shone with burnished copper linings.

"This is really beautiful," Darby couldn't help but comment as the hostess cheerfully showed them to a table.

"As long as they feed me," said Seth, apparently willing to let the topic of sleeping together drop.

She told herself she was glad to be back on safer ground. "I hear you," said Darby as she took her seat. "I skipped breakfast. Hadn't planned on also skipping lunch."

"You're not one of those women who starves herself."

"Hardly. Commercial flights don't serve food anymore. At least not to those of us who travel in economy."

"I wish I could get all affronted and tell you I fly economy all the time."

"But you don't."

"I don't," he admitted.

A waitress appeared and handed them each a leather-bound menu.

"You poor, cash-deprived rancher," she muttered.

If Seth heard, he didn't comment. Instead, he spoke to the waitress. "Do you happen to have Glen Klavit?"

"We do," the young woman answered brightly. "A single or a double?"

"Double." He looked to Darby.

"A lemon-drop martini," she decided. She'd already been up for twelve hours. Under normal circumstances, it would be early evening.

"That's the spirit," Seth approved. He looked to the waitress. "Can you bring us some bread or something to go with our drinks?"

"Coming right up. Do you need a few minutes with the menus?"

"We do."

With a friendly smile for Seth, she left.

There was a long moment of silence.

"You look very nice, you know," Seth commented, his gaze warm.

The glow of desire in her stomach moved to her chest, creating a decidedly dangerous tightness. "I thought we'd decided this wasn't a date."

"You told me I looked like a million bucks. I was just returning the compliment."

"I meant you had likely impressed the commission because you looked so much like them."

"You don't think you impressed them, too?"

"They took you more seriously."

"Why do you say that?" he asked, easing back in the padded leather chair. "I made my points. You made yours."

"Familiarity," she told him, opening the menu as a distraction from looking at him. "People are psychologically predisposed to agree with those who remind them of themselves, whether it's philosophically or physiologically."

"I bet you can't say that three times fast."

She met his gaze. "I'm serious."

"So am I. Go ahead, try it."

She wasn't about to take the bait. "When the members of the commission see you," she said instead, "they see themselves. When they see me, they see, well, not them."

"You think they're that shallow?"

"I think they, and you, don't even realize it's happening. The world is still organized around men: our governments, industry, the judiciary."

"There are plenty of female judges."

"A few," Darby allowed. "But trial and incarceration is an adversarial process, and that's how men typically frame the world. You can only win if the other side loses."

His brows drew together in puzzlement. "That's because one side is right and the other is wrong."

"Rarely," said Darby.

"We shouldn't jail convicted murderers?"

"We shouldn't jail victims of assault who fight back."

"We don't."

"We sure try."

Seth's cell phone rang, and he checked the number.

"Sorry." He glanced to Darby. "It's my brother, Travis." He answered the call as the waitress set down their drinks, along with a basket of assorted breads.

Seth's eyes went wide in obvious shock. *"What?"* he barked into the phone. "What exactly did you do?"

He listened, glancing at Darby.

She wondered if she should give him some privacy.

"Really? Well, I suppose you didn't have a choice, then."

She started to rise from her chair, but Seth waved her back.

"No," he said into the phone. "No, I get it. But I won't be back in Lyndon until later tonight."

Seth paused again. "I guess you will. Hang in there." He shook his head. "I know you have. Okay. Bye."

Darby knew she couldn't be rude enough to ask what was going on, but she was exceedingly curious.

"It's Travis," Seth offered without any prompting. "He's in jail."

That wasn't what she'd remotely expected to hear. Then again, she'd heard talk that Travis Jacobs could be hotheaded and impulsive. Of course, she'd never heard of him breaking the law.

"What did he do?" she asked.

"Ironically," said Seth, choosing a French roll from the basket, "he fought back."

"Someone assaulted him?"

"It was started by one of your disciples."

"I don't understand." She truly didn't.

"It seems a woman—I didn't catch her name—who agrees quite passionately with your perspective on the railway got into it with Joe Harry while having lunch at Maddy's Café.

Joe got agitated. Travis stepped in again to calm him down. Joe swung first, but Travis swung last. And the sheriff locked him up."

"Oh, no."

"Yeah." Seth sighed, leaning back in his chair. He took a sip of his scotch.

"Where's Joe Harry?" Darby asked. One would hope he'd be in jail along with Travis.

"In the hospital. It sounds like it's precautionary. The man's head is as hard as granite."

"Do we need to go back to Lyndon right away?"

"No rush. Travis will survive. Besides, he's the mayor's brother. The sheriff will probably let him out before too long."

"Is that a perk of being the mayor?" Darby couldn't help but ask.

Seth pushed the bread basket toward her. "Getting my brother out of jail?"

She helped herself to a triangle of herb cheese flatbread. "Having that kind of power."

"You think I'm interested in political power?"

"Many people are. It's a valid question."

"I ran for office to help the ranchers." Seth tore off a chunk of the roll.

"By having power as the mayor."

"No, by having an additional avenue through which to affect change."

"For the ranchers," she confirmed.

"For the citizens of Lyndon City."

"I'm a citizen of Lyndon City."

He flexed a grin. "You're a misguided citizen."

"That's too simple," she argued. "'I'm right and you're wrong?' You have to do better than that."

"I just presented a compelling case to the commission. You said so yourself."

"I said they were biased in your favor. You grew up on one of the biggest, wealthiest ranches in Lyndon Valley. You—"

"Where did you grow up?"

"Huh?" The abrupt change in topic surprised her.

"Where did you grow up?" he repeated, looking genuinely interested in the answer.

"Why?" She tried to figure out his angle. Was he going to contend that she didn't know Lyndon as well as he did?

"Quit being so suspicious. I'm not looking for secret information to throw back in your face. I'm trying to figure out what makes you tick."

"Fairness and equitability make me tick, particularly where it comes to gender bias. You had every economic and societal advantage growing up on a significant ranch in Lyndon Valley. Add to that, you're a man."

"What does that have to do with anything?"

"Ranches are organized around men, with women taking on supporting roles."

"They're organized around cattle. Where did you grow up? I'm thinking it wasn't a cattle ranch."

"New Jersey," she answered, seeing no reason to hide the truth. "I grew up in New Jersey."

"Not a lot of cows out there."

"No."

"My sister Mandy herds cattle. My sister Abigail deals with financial statements. And my sister Katrina left home to become a ballerina. Nobody was pigeonholed based on their gender."

"That's not my point."

"If your point is that it's an uneven world, then I don't disagree with you."

"So you admit I'm operating under a handicap?"

"Your biggest handicap is that more people in Lyndon want the railway than don't. If that wasn't true, you'd walk away with it, man, woman or Martian. Now, tell me about New Jersey."

She shrugged, letting the argument go. She was used to being able to debate people under the table. But Seth kept showing he had more stamina than she did. She needed to conserve her strength.

"Nothing much to tell," she answered. Her upbringing had been monotonous to say the least.

"What did your parents do there?"

"It was just my mom and me."

"Divorced?"

She wished. "One-night stand. I doubt he even used his real name. My mother was a cocktail waitress."

Seth's eyes turned sympathetic. "That sounds like a tough way to grow up."

"No worse than many other kids."

Darby didn't spend a lot of time dwelling on her childhood. She'd had a place to sleep, enough to eat and had gone to a decent school. She'd always felt a little out of step, especially in high school, when her classmates had decided that attracting boys was the only worthwhile endeavor. It was a relief to join the army, where miniskirts were never part of the dress code.

"Any sisters or brothers?" asked Seth.

"No. My mother got a lot more serious about birth control after I was born." Darby had been told many times that she was a mistake that had ruined her mother's life. "It was tough on her, being a single mom, always having to worry about a child. And I didn't exactly fit her mold. We were very different people, Roxanne and me."

"Different how?" His tone had gone unexpectedly soft.

"I was plain, practical, two feet firmly planted on the ground. She was beautiful, with a flair for the dramatic. I was punctual, good in the morning. She was action-seeking, great until three a.m. I liked order. She liked chaos."

Unexpectedly, his hand came out to cover hers. "I'm sorry to hear that."

"It was a long time ago." She couldn't help glancing at their joined hands.

"Do you still see her?"

Darby knew she should break their touch, but there was something strangely comforting in the feel of his warm palm. It wasn't arousing; simply strong and reassuring.

"She died last year," said Darby. "But we hadn't seen each other in a long time. Something about me going to college annoyed her, especially because the army paid for my education."

"That doesn't make sense."

"It did in her mind." It certainly wasn't Darby's favorite memory. "She said I should pull my own weight in the world. Like the military was an easy path."

"It was probably easier to cut you down than admit her own failings," Seth speculated.

"Roxanne Carroll, a failure? No. She had it all figured out. It was the rest of the world that didn't get it." Darby paused. "I don't know why I'm telling you all this."

She straightened and pulled her hand out from under his. She wasn't sure how the conversation had gotten so intimate. She liked to leave the past in the past.

The waitress appeared. "Are you ready to order?"

"I'd like a cheeseburger," said Darby, deciding that drinking a martini on an empty stomach wasn't going to turn out well. She didn't need to make any more childhood confessions to Seth.

"Sounds good," Seth echoed. "I'll take one, too."

With a quick check of their drinks, the woman left again.

"Sometimes it's good to get things off your chest," he offered.

"There's nothing to get off my chest. It was all a long time ago. And it wasn't all that terrible. It wasn't traumatic. It was more, well, tedious than anything else."

"Did you like the military?"

"I did." She took a sip of the tart martini.

"But you took a discharge."

"I decided I could do more from the outside."

"More to help your country?"

"And those in it."

There was a glint in his eye. "By teaching women to basket weave?"

She raised her glass in a mock toast. "Never underestimate the power of basket weaving. Sierra Hotel is about women doing what works for women on their very own terms."

Seth raised his own glass. "That sounds very noble."

She couldn't tell if he was mocking her. If he was, she refused to care. She was proud of her accomplishments, and completely convinced of her need to protect what she'd built.

"It is noble," she returned in an even tone, clinking her glass to his.

"I think I'm starting to like you, Darby."

"That's not a good idea, Seth."

But their gazes had become locked together, and neither seemed inclined to look away.

"We have to go back tonight," he said softly.

"I know we do." There was no way she could stay in Denver and explore her simmering feelings of desire. She didn't dare even acknowledge them, never mind encourage them.

"I want to stay," he told her.

She slowly shook her head. "You can't want that." Neither of them could want anything of the sort.

There was a long pause between them.

"What do you want?" he finally asked.

She determinedly stayed strong, refusing to let things soften between them. "What I've wanted all along. To win."

Travis's fistfight seemed to launch a wave of civil disobedience in Lyndon. The city's pro-railway signs were vandalized. Then, in apparent retaliation, someone spray-painted black lines on the banner that Darby and Marta had stretched from lightpost to lightpost across Main Street.

A few days later, there was a march through the town square in support of the railway. It was followed by a bigger march in opposition. Blogs sprung up, the debate raging on either side. The rhetoric got nasty, insults flying.

The referendum campaign was well under way when the local newspaper published an editorial defending the railway and urging voters to support it in the referendum. That night, a trash-can fire was lit on their porch. Luckily, the fire department arrived before it could do any real damage.

Then, Saturday night, in a local bar, the two factions squared off in a brawl that spilled out into the streets and sent six people to the hospital with cuts and bruises.

Frustrated, and growing genuinely concerned for public safety, Seth got up early Sunday and drove his way up to Sierra Hotel.

He'd kept his distance from Darby since Denver—because the more he was around her, the less he wanted to fight with her. The better he liked her, the more he wanted to understand her perspective. If he wasn't careful, he'd end up in a conflict of interest—the town's best interest versus his desire for Darby. Plus, if the public even suspected he had feelings for her, an already ugly situation could quickly spiral out of control.

He pulled into the parking lot of Sierra Hotel. There was a whole lot more activity around the property than the last time he'd been here. Six women were doing some kind of choreographed exercise in a meadow overlooking the lake. He was guessing it was Tai Chi. Another group of women was having breakfast on the deck at the side of the building, sitting in padded lounge furniture, engaging in what was obviously a spirited conversation.

Darby was on the deck. He stopped the truck, and she came to her feet, moving to the rail to watch the vehicle. When he exited the cab, and she recognized him, her brow furrowed. She quickly made her way to the staircase, trotting down to meet him.

When they drew close to each other on the driveway, she scanned his expression. "Something wrong?"

She was dressed in her typical worn khakis and a pair of practical, black sneakers. On top, she wore a blotchy, black-and-white tank. Her hair was pulled back in a loose braid, with a pair of aviator sunglasses perched on her nose.

She pulled the glasses up, sticking them into her hair as she gazed up at him. She looked breezy, unconcerned and ridiculously sexy. Her tank top fit snugly across her chest. She had amazing breasts, plump, round, perfectly shaped for the palm of his hand.

"Did you hear about the fight last night?" he asked without preamble.

"Travis again?" she asked.

"No, not Travis. Is there somewhere we can talk privately?"

She frowned. "Is the fight a secret?"

"It's a complication. There were a lot of people involved, but there's something I need to ask you." He glanced at her front door. "Inside, maybe?"

"We can't talk out here?"

He was trying to be circumspect, in light of her guests. He didn't want to disrupt their vacations. Then again, what had happened last night was no secret.

"There was a brawl at the Hound and Hen. Six people wound up in the hospital."

Her brow creased. "Please tell me it wasn't about the railway."

"It was about the railway," he confirmed. "You must have heard about the vandalism and the fire."

She nodded, looking more worried by the moment.

"I think we can agree this is getting out of hand."

"Sad that it took this for us to agree." But even as she gave him that unguarded opinion, she was moving toward the front door.

"We agreed on motherhood and apple pie," he reminded her.

"Everyone agrees on motherhood and apple pie. Are they going to be okay?"

He fell into step. "Eventually. It's mostly cuts and bruises."

"What sparked it? Who started it?"

"You've amassed a loyal following," he observed.

"And you haven't? It's encouraging that so many people are choosing tranquility over industrial development."

"I didn't have to amass them. The majority was on board with the railway all along. That's why they voted for me."

She stopped halfway up the short staircase, turning to meet him at eye level. "Are you blaming me for a barroom brawl?"

"I'm not sure whether to blame you or admire you," he answered honestly. "You've turned this into one hell of a horse race."

She took the last couple of steps backward, as if she wanted to keep an eye on him. She reached behind her to turn the doorknob, pushing the door wide open. "I never intended for anyone to get hurt."

"I know you didn't," he allowed.

The inside of the building was cool and bright, light from a glass wall flooded into the great room. He noticed the furniture was oversized, leather and extremely comfortable looking. The couches and chairs were earth tones, arranged in small groupings around a central, stone fireplace.

The ceilings were high, with massive cedar beams arching across the room. A natural wood staircase led from the entry to an open hallway along the second floor with six doors leading off.

"My office is through the kitchen," she said, leading him past an island, past the freshly painted alcove, along a short hallway and through a door to a bright, octagonal room.

It had a multitude of windows and several skylights. Opaque blinds on the lower windows provided privacy, but it remained bright and cheerful. A maple desk with a computer, guest chairs and bookshelves took up one corner. A small meeting table was centrally located. Darby bypassed them all, leading the way to a sofa with a pair of matching armchairs facing it across a glass-topped coffee table.

She took one of the armchairs, while he took the other.

"This is nice," he complimented, feeling very much at home in the room.

"Thank you." She paused. "Ironic that you're setting out to destroy it."

"This has never been about you, or about Sierra Hotel," he couldn't help but put in. If he could support the town and make her happy at the same time, he'd do it in a heartbeat.

"Funny, it feels like it's always been about me." She kicked off her running shoes and pulled one leg up beneath her in the big chair.

She looked vulnerable, beautiful and so incredibly sexy that his breath stalled in his chest. He didn't want to defeat her. He wanted to protect her. He wanted to hold her safe in his arms and keep the entire world at bay.

"So, what now?" she asked, unfastening her braid, raking back her hair with spread fingers and refastening it into a ponytail.

He watched her movements, remembering the softness of her hair between his fingertips, the feel of her lithe body in his arms, the taste of her lips on his.

"Seth?"

He shook himself back to reality. "I need your help."

She coughed a short laugh. "Why am I skeptical?"

"We need to do something about the rhetoric. The debate. The escalating arguments."

"I'll take care of my arguments. You're on your own."

He shook his head. "I don't mean you should help me frame them. I want you to help me stop them."

"Why would I do that?"

"Because there are some very impassioned people in this town."

"Yeah?" She cocked her head sideways. "That sounds like the mayor's job to me."

"Agreed. But for better or worse, you and I are the ones

setting the example, and I think for everybody's sake we need to dial it back."

She dropped her hands into her lap, looking suspicious and skeptical. "You're asking me to back off? Back off from pushing my side of the referendum?"

"You agreed that things are getting out of hand."

"I did. But dialing it back helps your side, not mine. You said it yourself, your supporters are already your supporters. I'm the one with ground to make up."

He struggled to hold his frustration in check. "You think I'm asking to gain an advantage? Six people went to the hospital last night."

"I will concede, as mayor, you probably also want to stop the public fistfights."

"As mayor, or as anybody else, that's exactly what I want to do. Quite frankly, at this point, that's *all* I want to do." Swaying voters on the referendum was going to have to wait until the peace returned to Lyndon.

"Don't pretend you haven't thought about the spin-offs of this plan for your side of the debate. I can see them already, and I've only been thinking about it for two minutes."

"I think you're better than me at gauging the angles."

"Don't give me that 'aw shucks, ma'am' response and pretend you just wandered in off the back forty. It won't make me let my guard down."

"I'm not pretending anything. This is how my brain is working." He counted on his fingers. "Step one, stop the bar fights. Step two, worry about the referendum. And that's it. Maybe you can do five things at once, but I'm a sequential guy. I want my city to be safe. And if you have a better idea of how to make it safe, I'm all ears."

She paused, obviously considering his perspective. As she should, because he was right. Their best possible move was to tone down their own argument. They needed to set an example. If the two of them demonstrated restraint and calm, there was a chance their supporters would follow suit.

"How would that work?" she finally asked.

He tried not to let the relief show in his expression. "You and I would be cordial, friendly and respectful."

She blew out a skeptical breath. "You and me? We may have to practice a bit to get to that."

"No shouting," he elaborated. "No name-calling—"

"I never—"

"No eye rolls, no dismissive gestures, no sarcastic contradictions."

"I'm serious." She sat forward in her chair. "If we want to pull that off, we're going to have to practice."

"You don't think you can control yourself?"

"I don't think either of us can control ourselves. You know what we're like when we get together."

It was on the tip of his tongue to tell her he wished he did. There wasn't a thing in the world he'd like better than getting together with Darby, in every possible sense of the phrase.

"That's not what I meant." She correctly interpreted his expression. But her hands had tightened on the arms of the chair, and her eyes had turned opaque with what looked like desire.

Her posture and expression sent his libido into overdrive. He gathered his self-control and lowered his tone. "That might not be what you meant. But it's something else we better worry about. Nobody can know about this thing we've got—"

"There is no thing."

"Oh, yes, there is." He knew enough to realize that the attraction between them was a complicating factor. They had to keep it firmly in check, not let a hint of it sneak out. "You look at me with those bedroom eyes."

"I don't have bedroom eyes. Leave my eyes out of this."

"We need to be careful."

"I'm not worried," she retorted.

"I am."

"I'm not likely to throw myself in your arms in front of an audience." But her expression said she was thinking about it.

"If you look at me like that, you won't have to."

...ertainly. Again, respectfully. While I do understand ...e people's desire for corporate profit above quality of ..."

"Careful," Seth warned.

"What careful?"

"That's very loaded language."

"I was merely stating a fact," Darby pointed out.

"Quality of life can be enhanced by increased job oppor- ...unities. And improving the economy will increase job op- ...ortunities—"

"That's not a certainty."

"It's a very high-percentage probability."

Her irritation inched upward. "Noise pollution and com- promises to public safety are not a high-percentage probabil- ity. They are a certainty."

"Loaded language again," he warned.

"More facts," she countered.

"Do you want to take money out of the pockets of ranch- ers, and therefore food out of the mouths of their children?"

Now that was over the top. "You have got to be kidding me."

"If you can use loaded language, so can I."

"Starving children, Seth? Really?"

"I can also link my standpoint to motherhood, apple pie and puppies."

Okay, he wasn't the only one who could take his argument ...o ridiculous lengths. "Trains kill puppies."

"Oh, you're going to have to back that one up with sta- ...istics."

Darby rocked to her feet and moved to her computer table. ...urely she could validate the argument. She heard Seth move ...o behind her.

"Finding anything?" he asked, his deep voice in her left ...r.

"Give me a minute." She scrolled through the results. "Doesn't look promising."

"You mean they'll figure it out for themselves?"

"I mean, I'll grab you and carry you out the nearest exit."

"Ha, ha."

"I'm not joking. It's a fight for me to keep from kissing you right now."

A slight flush rose on her cheeks, making her look even more desirable. "You can't just up and kiss me, Seth."

"You can up and kiss me," he told her softly and honestly. "Any old time you want. I won't mind in the least."

She didn't seem to have a comeback for that.

Instead, her jaw dropped ever so slightly. Her lips were dark and full. And as she blinked, he watched her lashes sweep across her gorgeous, moss-green eyes.

Seth crooked his finger, motioning her toward him.

She gave a very subtle shake of her head.

But he knew he was right. His voice went lower, husky with desire. "We should get it out of our system."

A few moments passed in absolute silence.

"That's a ridiculous plan."

"You got a better one?" He eased forward in the chair. "Because, if you do, I'm all for it."

"We ignore the attraction."

"Tried that. Only made it worse."

She didn't answer. If he had to guess, he'd say she was stunned into silence.

"Can you stop thinking about me?" he dared to ask.

She still didn't answer.

He reached for her hand. It felt warm, soft, delicate in his own. "If we let it keep bubbling under the surface, it's going to explode at the worst possible moment."

"Nothing's bubbling anywhere."

"Yes, it is." He tugged her forward.

"Seth, please."

He stopped pulling on her, but he didn't let go of her hand. "Can you get through a day without thinking about me?" he repeated.

"No," she admitted, with what looked like annoyance. "I can't."

He knew this was the time for sincerity. It was the only thing they hadn't tried yet, and he needed to shake things up.

"Is it getting worse for you?" he asked. "Because it's sure getting worse for me."

She glanced at their joined hands. "This isn't the answer."

"Diffusing the tension is the only answer."

Her mouth quirked in a reluctant grin. "I'm not going to kiss you again, Seth."

"Give me another answer."

"We're adults. We ignore it."

He stroked his thumb along her palm. "And when that stops working?" He gazed deeply into her eyes. "What then?"

"By then, the referendum will be over."

"You think we can hold out for fifty-three days?" He wasn't sure he could hold out for fifty-three minutes.

"Let's practice," she suggested, pulling her hand away from his.

"Practice not sleeping together?"

Her expression faltered for a split second. "I meant practice discussing the railway without shouting and name-calling."

Six

For a moment, Seth looked like he was going to argue, bu to her surprise, he didn't. Instead, he settled casually bac in the armchair, crossing one ankle over the opposite kne "Sure, Darby. Let's practice."

Unfortunately, he looked ridiculously sexy lounging in office. She wanted to think about the railroad, but it was much easier to think about his kisses.

"Uh...I...okay." She swallowed, while he cracked a kr ing smile.

It was what she needed to focus her thoughts. "Wit respect, Mr. Mayor," she told him evenly and carefully, out inflection, "Lyndon Valley has thrived for decade without the benefit of a railroad."

"With due respect, Ms. Carroll," his tone was equal "improvements are improvements, even if they are time in coming."

"And sacrifices are sacrifices."

"Perhaps you would be so kind as to enumer sacrifices."

Send For
2 FREE BOOKS
Today!

I accept your offer!

Please send me two free Harlequin® Desire® novels and two mystery gifts (gifts worth about $10). I understand that these books are completely free—even the shipping and handling will be paid—and I am under no obligation to purchase anything, ever, as explained on the back of this card.

225/326 HDL F43T

Please Print

FIRST NAME

LAST NAME

ADDRESS

APT.#   CITY

STATE/PROV.   ZIP/POSTAL CODE

Visit us online at
www.ReaderService.com

He was right. There were apparently no documented cases of trains killing puppies.

"Well, for sure they kill mothers," said Darby.

"Maybe if the villain ties her to the railroad tracks."

Darby turned, keeping a straight face. "We can't discount that happening."

"I bet those horrible trains squish apple pies, as well." He smirked.

She shook her head. "We seem to have gotten off track."

"Pun intended?"

"Not really," she admitted.

"You're right," he agreed, surprising her. "This isn't helping."

She searched his expression for sarcasm. But he looked genuinely regretful. He also looked handsome, and so irredeemably sexy that her hormones sang in response to his nearness. She could feel her heartbeats grow deeper and a flush of heat race its way along her skin.

"We kind of blew that, didn't we?" he observed.

"You want to take it from the top?"

Though she hadn't admitted it to Seth, she was growing quite worried about the mood of the town. She didn't want any more fights or vandalism, and she accepted the wisdom of her and Seth's setting an example.

"Sure," he agreed, easing ever so slightly forward. "Let's take it from the top."

Her gaze found its way to his lips, and her voice turned husky as she spoke. "I respect your right to disagree with me."

"And I respect your right to disagree with me." The back of his hand brushed lightly against hers.

She swallowed, but forced herself to keep going. "I know you want what's best for Lyndon City."

"That's good," he intoned. His hand brushed hers again, and her brain started to cloud. "I know you love puppies."

"I do love puppies," she agreed, meeting his darkening eyes.

"I love warm brandy," he returned.

"Chocolate chip cookies," she breathed.

"Midnight swims." The palm of his hand came to rest on her hip.

She knew she should move away. It was crazy to simply stand here and let him touch her. But instead, she added to his last sentence. "On hot, summer nights."

His head slanted sideways, leaning in. "Naked," he whispered.

"Uh-oh."

"With you." His mouth came down on hers.

He tasted astonishingly familiar, intense, compelling. He shifted his body, meeting hers from thigh to chest. His arms settled around her waist, while hers snaked around his neck, tightening.

She tipped her head back, opening her mouth, letting the sweep of his tongue send ripples of desire along her limbs. She welcomed the invasion of his kiss, her skin rising up in goose bumps, her nipples tightening with pent-up desire.

Their kisses went on and on. Her spine arched backward. Her fingers tangled in his short hair. His hand slid up her rib cage, skimming the side of her breast, then palming its fullness and closing in on her hard nipple.

"You're gorgeous," he breathed. "So soft, so smooth."

She was also very much out of her mind. She knew she should put a stop to this right now. She had no business melting in the arms of her enemy. But she didn't have it in her to stop. She didn't have it in her to say no.

His kisses were mind-blowing. His hands were nothing short of magic. And she'd dreamed about this for so many nights. Surely she could simply enjoy the intense sensations a little while longer. How much could it hurt?

His hand slipped under her tank top, calluses teasing her sensitized skin. His hands were warm and strong, firm and sure. His fingertips found the thin lace of her bra, zeroing in on her nipple, and a primal groan formed deep in his throat.

His breathing was deep. He gathered the hem of her top, bunching it. She raised her arms, allowing him to peel it off. He stared hotly at her white bra for a long, still moment. Then he smoothed back her hair, captured her lips with his, and kissed her all over again.

She clung to him, burying her face in the crook of his neck, inhaling his spicy scent as the air currents swirled across her bare back. He snapped her bra open, tossing it aside. He shrugged out of his jacket and made short work of the buttons on his dress shirt.

Then they were skin to skin, her breasts pressed up against his chest, heat, friction and moisture rising between them. He smoothed his palms along her bare back, kneading her muscles with the heels of his hands. He kissed the arc of her shoulder, working his way along the curve of her neck, back to her mouth, devouring her with deep, long kisses.

She explored his bared torso, the six-pack of his abs, the definition of his pecs, the breadth of his shoulders, bunched steel under her fingers. She stretched up to kiss his neck, tasting the salt tang, suckling his heated skin, while her hands stroked the expanse of his back.

He lifted her, perching her on the table, stepping between her thighs. His head bent to draw one nipple into his mouth. The heat and moisture made her gasp. His tongue was rough and sure. She arched for him, gripping his shoulders, as he stroked her sensitized skin. Waves of desire built within her, peaking to crests, meeting between her thighs.

She dragged oxygen into her lungs, inarticulate moans rising from the tension in her chest. Her thighs tightened around him as she pressed herself against his aroused body.

"Seth," she gasped.

He lifted his head, eyes smoke-blue, glazed with arousal. He seemed to blink her into focus. His hands gripped the table on either side of her.

"If it's a no," he rasped, "better tell me now."

"It's not a no," she managed. She lifted her hand to his cheek. It was trembling slightly from the effects of her passion.

She stroked his strong jawline, tunneled her fingers into his hair. "You're not…" She didn't know how to finish the sentence. He kept surprising her. He wasn't what she expected.

"Neither are you," he said softly.

Then he met her lips, gently at first, then hotter and deeper, starting the raw, ravaging kisses all over again.

His hand skimmed her stomach, moving to her waistband, releasing the button of her slacks and dragging down the zipper, stripping them off. His fingertips caressed her bare hips, her thighs, moving to the apex, until he met her moisture.

He lingered there, and she arched her spine. He pressed his fingers inside, bracing her bottom with his free hand, moving in and out until she squirmed against the tabletop, biting her bottom lip.

Something banged in the yard outside. The sound was followed by shrieks and giggles.

Seth jerked back, eyes wide as he stared down at her.

"Do not stop," Darby ground out from between clenched teeth. "Don't you dare stop."

"Yes, ma'am." His hand continued its motion.

She let her arousal build as high as she dared.

"Now," she cried out. And it was her turn to grip the edge of the table as he shucked his own pants and retrieved a condom from his pocket.

He was gorgeous naked, tough, toned, tanned and glorious. Their gazes locked together as he stepped forward.

For a split second, sanity took a toehold inside Darby's brain. Marta's cool tones echoed through her memory.

She moistened her lips, struggling to find her voice. "Would this be a good time to ask you to cancel the railroad?"

Seth's mouth flexed in a crooked smile, and he grasped her thighs, easing them farther apart as his thumbs slid up their slickness, meeting in the middle. "Would this be a good time to ask you to endorse the railroad?"

She gasped in a breath, and her hips reflexively bucked. "Yes."

He bracketed her hips and slid her to him, holding her precariously on the edge of the table. "Then let's both let each other off the hook."

He bent to her lips in an openmouthed kiss, simultaneously sinking inside her. She wrapped her arms around him, sliding their moist bodies tight together. Her ankles locked as his rhythm started, his hand cupping her bottom, stretching her body, hitting every erotic nerve ending she possessed.

"Seth," she gasped.

"Darby," he groaned in return.

Sensation inched its way through her body, slow-motion intensity buzzing from her core to her limbs to her fingers and toes.

"This is—" she gasped, feeling as though she was losing her grip on reality. "It can't—"

"I know." His voice was guttural between kisses. "It's nothing to do with anything else. We can't use it against each other."

"We can't," she agreed.

His pace increased, slamming fireworks to every corner of her body. A roaring started in her ears. Orange sparks turned to a glow behind her eyes. Her world contracted to Seth, his heat, his scent, his shallow breaths, to where their bodies joined.

She struggled to stay silent. There were other people in the building. But she lost the battle, crying out as lightning jolts of pleasure flashed through her body, convulsing her around Seth.

He covered her mouth with his own, absorbing her cries. Then his body shuddered with completion, and he squeezed her to him, lifting her right off the table, gasping her name over and over in her ear.

* * *

Seth blinked the world back into focus, gazing dazedly into Darby's beautiful face. He couldn't believe he'd done it. He couldn't believe *they'd* done it. He'd all but torn off their clothes, making frantic love to her in the middle of her office, in the middle of the day, in what was essentially a public building. They hadn't even locked the damn door.

"That—" Darby sucked in a few gasping breaths "—may not have been a good idea."

The jury was still out for Seth. It was likely a very bad idea, but he couldn't deny that he felt fantastic. His world felt completely centered for the first time in months.

"I know I feel a lot less tense and antsy," he told her, gently easing her down to rest on the table.

"I guess I do, too," she agreed, her luminous green eyes gazing up into his. "At least for the moment."

He couldn't bring himself to let her go, so he tightened his arms around her and kept their bodies firmly locked. He didn't want to lose any of the sensations wafting through his brain: her warm, supple limbs, the sweet scent of her hair, the exotic taste of her skin.

He kissed the closest spot, the top of her head, while his fingertips stroked the length of her back. "You know, I think we might have hit on something here."

She didn't push him away. In fact, her body seemed to soften around him. He reveled in the stolen moments, even as reality percolated its way back into his brain.

"How so?" she asked softly against his chest.

"I don't feel like fighting," he observed. "Do you feel like fighting?"

She gave a weak laugh. "My brain went blank about fifteen minutes ago."

Seth couldn't help but like the sound of that. Because, for sure, she'd blown every circuit in his own brain. He couldn't remember ever wanting a woman this way. He sure didn't remember sex completely blotting out all time, space and reason.

"Darby—" he stroked her hair back "—I can understand why you'd prefer to maintain the peace and tranquility of Lyndon Valley."

She stilled, silent for a dozen heartbeats. "Seth," she said softly, and there was a thread of a smile in her voice. "I understand why you think the train is a good idea."

She tipped her head back to look up at him.

He smiled. "There you have it."

"Have what?"

"The next time we're scheduled to debate in public, let's do this first."

"You mean rock each other's world?"

"If you want to put it that way."

She laughed, dropping her forehead to rest against his chest. "You're out of your mind."

"It's the only thing we've found that works."

She shook her head against him, pulling back. "You don't particularly like me, really."

Something contracted inside Seth's chest, leaving him feeling hollow, regretful. "I like you, Darby," he told her softly. "I disagree with you, and I'm a little intimidated by you. But I like you just fine."

"I don't intimidate you," she stated with conviction.

How wrong she was there.

Then curiosity crept into her tone. "How do I intimidate you?"

The air was cooling their damp skin. Sounds from outside, a voice, a bird, the wind, began to filter into the room.

"You're smart," Seth told her, easing slightly away. "You're feisty. If I dare to make one wrong move, you pounce like a puma."

He reached to the floor, handing her the bra and tank top.

"You intimidate me back," she told him. "You're a brick wall. And if I'm not careful, I'll break myself against you."

She took the clothing he handed her, shrugging into the white, lacy bra.

His brain took a snapshot of the acutely sexy picture, filing it away for later. She was beyond incredible, all smooth, honey-toned skin, mussed hair, swollen lips.

She pulled the tank top over her head and slid down from the table.

Seth stepped into his pants, while she did the same.

He supposed it was way too much to hope that she'd make love with him ever again. This had been a misstep, a momentary anomaly. Mind-blowing sex notwithstanding, they couldn't afford to trust each other.

They were about to step back into their corners and come out swinging. If he was lucky, if Lyndon City was really lucky, they'd find a way to pull their punches.

Darby lay in bed alone that night debating the merits of Seth's proposition. On the one hand, she could have a lot more great sex with him. On the other hand, it was inappropriate to mix a physical relationship up in their dispute.

She knew what was right. But she also knew what she wanted. And she dozed off to the memory of Seth's sure hands caressing every inch of her body.

A booming sound awoke her. Her feet hit the floor before she'd even identified the sound.

It boomed again.

"What the hell?" Darby asked to the empty room.

It sounded like a twelve-gauge shotgun. And it was close, maybe fifty yards away.

An air horn pierced the darkness, long and shrill.

Darby gave her head a little shake, allowing for the possibility that she was dreaming. If she was, she really did prefer those dreams that centered around an illicit relationship with Seth.

Two more booms sounded, followed by another air horn blast.

It was obvious they weren't hitting the inn. If somebody wanted to shoot up Sierra Hotel, a shotgun was a colossally stupid choice of weapon.

Voices stirred up in the other bedrooms.

Darby moved to the door and pulled it open.

"Everybody stay down," she called down the hallway. "Stay in your rooms."

"You need help?" came a voice she recognized as Shelley, an L.A. police officer.

"Call 911."

"Those were gunshots," someone called back.

"I don't think they're aiming at us," Darby returned. "But stay down, okay?"

A number of voices called back in agreement.

Darby pulled on a pair of runners, making her way carefully to the front foyer in a pair of soft blue shorts and a yellow tank top. The horn continued to sound, and the shotgun blasts stayed intermittent. But they seemed to be getting closer.

The sounds were coming from the north, where there was a strip of woods beyond the lawn. Whoever it was could be hiding there.

She eased the front door open a few inches.

"Police are on their way," called a voice over the rail.

"Thanks," Darby called back. "Stay away from the windows."

"We are."

Darby heard a voice, then another. Whoops and hollers combined with swearwords.

Darby mentally cataloged her guests, wondering if any of them might possibly be an assassination target. She didn't think so, but any one of them could be involved in espionage or counterintelligence without her knowing it.

Then again, what self-respecting assassin brought a shotgun and an air horn to a hit? Nothing about the situation made sense.

It was too dark for hunting, and way too noisy for vandalism. Then a lightbulb clicked on in Darby's head.

It was sound vandalism. The air horn was supposed to mimic a train.

The shotgun went silent, and the air horn seemed to peter out. Darby strained to hear. She could barely make out voices.

She moved onto the porch, sidling along the wall, staying in the shadows.

"Is it jammed?" one male voice asked, and she realized they were hidden behind her shed.

"Probably out of air," came another.

Darby realized they sounded young, maybe midteens.

She heard the faint sound of sirens in the distance.

One of the boys swore.

"Run for it!" called the other.

Darby took a chance. "Hold it right there," she called in a no-nonsense, captain voice.

Silence.

"I've got you covered," she lied. "Put down the gun and come out."

There were mutters of uncertainty from behind the shed.

"Do it now!" she demanded.

"Don't shoot," came the response.

"We're coming out."

Two teenage boys rounded the sidewall of the shed, arms dramatically in the air, eyes as big as saucers.

"What the hell are you *doing?*" Darby demanded, staying back far enough that they couldn't tell if she was holding a firearm.

"It was just a joke," one of them responded in a shaky, somewhat slurred voice, making it obvious they'd been drinking.

"You could have killed someone," said Darby.

"We weren't even pointin' at you," the kid protested, tone turning surly.

"You don't know what you were pointing at," she told them. "It's dark. You can't even see who's out here."

"You should have stayed in the house."

"You should have stayed home in bed," she returned.

The sirens grew louder, and flashing lights appeared on the horizon.

"Why'd you call the cops?" one of the boys demanded.

"Let me see.... Because you were shooting at us."

"Not *at* you."

"We were just making a little noise. Making a point."

"That point have something to do with the railroad?" Darby asked with disgust.

Their mulish expressions answered her question.

The headlights of two squad cars and a third vehicle bounced their way up the driveway, pulling up to the inn. The boys stayed frozen in place.

"We're so screwed," one of them muttered.

"Told ya we should have run for it."

The officers exited their cars and swiftly cuffed the boys. To Darby's surprise, the third car contained Seth. He strode past the teenagers, staring hard at them as he made his way straight to her.

"You all right?" Seth asked.

"Fine. They were just making noise."

"I recognized them. They're in very deep trouble."

He was dressed in a worn, gray T-shirt and a pair of faded blue jeans over scuffed cowboy boots. His hair was slightly messy, and he looked like he'd just rolled out of bed.

"Tell me what happened."

"What are you doing here?"

"When they heard it was your place, they called."

Darby went on alert. "Why?"

"Because of the railway vandalism. Why would you think?"

"No reason."

"So tell me what happened."

"We woke up to air horn and shotgun blasts."

Seth glanced to where the two handcuffed teenagers were being led away by the uniformed police. Their shoulders and heads were bent. It was obvious they were having second thoughts about the stunt they'd pulled.

"At first I thought they were shooting at Sierra Hotel, though I was pretty sure none of the shots were hitting the building. So I went outside to investigate."

"You went outside?" Seth interrupted.

"Yes."

"To investigate gunfire?" he asked incredulously.

"And an air horn. We figured anyone trying to sneak up and kill us would have skipped the air horn and come a little closer to the building before deploying the twelve gauge."

"You got them to surrender?"

"They were hiding behind the shed. I ordered them to come out, and they did."

"What if they'd shot you?"

"They didn't. They told me it was a joke, that they weren't shooting at the inn. They were just trying to make a little noise." She gave Seth a pointed stare. "Train-type noise."

"Are you *kidding* me?" he asked.

"Do I look like I'm kidding you?"

"This is off the charts."

"You're telling me."

With the teenagers in the backseat, one of the officers approached. "Can you come down to the station tomorrow morning?" he asked Darby.

"Sure," she agreed, wanting nothing more than to crawl back into bed at the moment.

"Thank you, ma'am." He tipped his hat. "Mayor."

"Thanks, Peterson," Seth returned.

The officer made a hand signal, and they started the squad cars, pulling back down the driveway.

"I'm staying," Seth said.

Darby turned to gape at him. "What?"

"There's no way I'm leaving you up here all by yourself."

"I have ten guests."

"So what?"

"So I'm not alone."

"Are your guests going to help you when the next guy shows up with a rifle?"

"Nobody's showing up with a rifle." Though Darby wished she could tell Seth one of her guests was a SWAT-team member. Maybe that would put his mind at ease.

The front door opened, and the guests spilled out. "Darby?"

"Be right there," she called to them. "Everything's fine."

"I'm going to stay," Seth repeated.

She put a hand on his arm. "And tell people what?"

"I don't have to tell them anything."

"You'll have to explain to your supporters why you spent the night with your archenemy."

"I'll sleep on the couch."

"Oh, that'll fix it. Because crazy rumor and speculation never happens in this town."

"We have witnesses."

"Darby?" one of the guests asked again.

She turned her head. "Shelley, can you put the kettle on?"

"Sure." The women retreated back into the inn.

"I'll stay for tea," said Seth.

"We're having hot chocolate."

"Even better."

"Go home, Seth. Remember what happened with Joe? We absolutely need your supporters to know you're with them. If they think you've betrayed them by fraternizing with me, who knows what'll happen next."

He hesitated, then raked his hand through his short hair. "I don't like this."

"I don't, either," she agreed.

"You call me if anything else happens."

"I'll call 911."

"Me. You call me." He sucked in a breath, his hand covering hers where it rested on his arm. "Okay, you can call 911, too."

"It's not your responsibility. It's not your fault."

He looked deeply into her eyes. "It feels like my fault." He paused. "Darby—"

"No." She shook her head. "Don't say anything else."

Seven

Despite the interruption, Darby's guests enjoyed the next three days of their stay at Sierra Hotel. And overtop of Marta's objections, Darby put some focus on toning down the railway rhetoric. They revised the website and sent a letter to the editor in favor of civil debate and discourse, talking about the fairness of the referendum process and encouraging people to vote.

Though everyone in Lyndon knew about the shotgun and air horn incident, and many of the anti-railway faction were incensed by it, Darby hoped she'd done her part to tone things down. At the end of the week, the guests departed.

With the rooms all cleaned, and no new guests due for several days, Darby gave her four staff members some time off. No sooner had they all left, and she'd curled up in the great room with a promising biography, than a vehicle pulled up in the driveway.

Disappointed, she rolled to her feet, making her way to the door, hoping it wasn't a tourist looking for a room to rent.

She hated to turn people away, but she wasn't in the business of general tourism.

Out on the porch, she was surprised to see Abigail Rainer and her two sisters, Mandy and Katrina, getting out of the car.

"You said to come by and see the place," Abigail called with a wave as they crossed the gravel turnaround. "Is this a bad time?"

"Not at all," Darby replied, hurrying down to meet them, quickly deciding her reading could wait. This would be a golden opportunity to present her case to Seth's three sisters.

"This is gorgeous," said Katrina, craning her elegant neck to take in the front of the building. She wore detailed jeans and a white silk blouse. "How long has the bigger building been here?"

"I've been working on it for a couple of years now."

When Darby inherited the property from her great-aunt, the roomy house had needed repairs. In order to turn it into Sierra Hotel, Darby had constructed an addition. The building was now six or seven times the original size.

Mandy joined them beside the SUV. She was dressed far more casually than her younger sister, in blue jeans and a blue flannel shirt, her chestnut hair pulled back in a ponytail.

"It reminds me of how long it's been since I was up here," she said. "I got along well with your aunt."

"That's good to know," Darby acknowledged. "I only met her a couple of times, and I was pretty young."

"Seriously?" Mandy asked.

"My mom wasn't close to her family."

"So this must have come as quite a surprise," said Katrina.

"A good surprise," said Darby.

Abigail arched her back against the weight of her protruding belly. "I absolutely love the deck."

"There's a bigger one out back," said Darby. "It has a fantastic view of the lake."

She motioned to the front porch. "If you'd like to see it, we can cut through the inn."

While Mandy and Katrina chatted and walked ahead of them, Abigail fell into step beside Darby. "Seth seems worried about you," she opened.

The statement took Darby by surprise. She hadn't expected Seth to mention her to his family—other than to complain.

"Worried how?" she asked Abigail.

"He doesn't like the mood of the city. He's uncomfortable about your guests leaving, and you being alone up here."

Darby paused. "He knows my guests left?"

Was Seth keeping some kind of tabs on her?

"He's the mayor," said Abigail. "They would have flown out through the airport, right?"

"And by what legal mechanism does he access airline manifests? Or my guest register, for that matter? What did he do, compare the two?"

The night of the shootings, Darby had found Seth's concern endearing. But now it sounded slightly underhanded.

"I think it's more likely the airport manager called him when your van pulled up with ten women boarding flights."

"So he has spies, then?"

Abigail was smiling. "It's a small town."

Darby reminded herself that she was supposed to be cozying up to Abigail, not challenging her. No matter what had happened, her quarrel was with Seth, not his sister.

She quickly backed off. "I'm sorry. I have no reason to be angry."

"No need to be sorry. But honestly, I think the fact that he's worried about you being up here all alone is more interesting than how he got the information."

"Well, he can keep his worry to himself. I'm perfectly fine."

"Okay to go in?" Mandy called from the porch.

"Yes, please. Go ahead." Darby started walking again.

"That was a bit of a knee jerk," Abigail observed, her tone mild.

Darby mounted the staircase. "Letting them go inside?"

"Assuming Seth was up to no good."

Darby had good reason for the reaction. "Believe me, I've learned a little bit about him over the past few weeks."

"I lived with him for a couple of decades."

Once again, Darby regretted her words to Abigail. "I didn't mean—"

"Are you attracted to my brother?"

Darby bought herself a minute to think by moving single file through the doorway. Mandy and Katrina were already inside, oohing and aahing over the stone fireplace.

"If I said no," Darby ventured quietly, "I'd be protesting too much. Because your brother is an exceedingly attractive man. If I said yes, you're going to take it the wrong way. Because it's not what you'd think."

"What do I think?" Abigail asked with a knowing smile.

"That I have some kind of an emotional reaction to Seth beyond sex."

"Sex?"

"I mean sex appeal, of course."

"You said sex."

"He's a sexy guy," Darby allowed, deciding to give Abigail a little bit of what she was looking for. "I've fantasized about him."

Abigail's eyes glowed with mischievous satisfaction. "And I'll bet he's fantasized about you."

Darby knew that he had. He'd flat out told her so.

"I'm not the thought police," she told Abigail airily. "He can fantasize however he likes."

"How many bedrooms?" Katrina called, gazing up the wide, polished-pine staircase.

"Ten guest rooms upstairs," said Darby, happy for an excuse to get out of the conversation with Abigail. "They each have their own bathroom."

"I hear this is just for women," Mandy put in.

"Just for women," Darby confirmed. "It's a nice retreat

from the pressures of life, where women can kick back on their own and take it easy for a few days."

Katrina motioned to the stairway, a question mark in her expression.

Darby nodded. "Go ahead. They've just been cleaned."

"We should come for a stay up here," Mandy put in, following Katrina. "Us and Lisa. She's our cousin," Mandy added, obviously for Darby's benefit.

"Sure," Darby agreed. Then she stepped straight into the issue. "Assuming I'm able to stay open."

"Would you really shut it down?" asked Abigail, as her two sisters trotted up the stairs.

"I'd have no choice. I can't afford to start over somewhere else. And what I'm trying to do won't work here with the kind of disruption the trains will bring."

"It's only a few trains a day."

"To start. But it's definitely going to increase over time. And that doesn't count the two years of construction, when there'll be almost constant noise and activity. I can't make it two years with no customers."

"Seth knows this?"

Darby gave a helpless laugh. "If he doesn't, he's even better at denial than I thought."

"You just did it again," said Abigail.

"Did what?" Darby was confused.

"There's a lilt in your voice when you talk about him."

"Must be a result of that midnight fantasy." Darby answered quickly, starting for the stairs to cover her astonishment at Abigail's powers of observation. "Come on up. Most of the rooms have balconies, and the views are amazing."

Abigail followed behind. "He does it, too."

"I put oversize, jetted tubs in each of the en suites," Darby rattled on. "And each of the rooms comes with a wine rack."

"When he talks about you," Abigail continued. "There's something in his tone that—"

"Are you here to check out Sierra Hotel or me?" Darby interrupted, pausing at the top of the stairs.

Abigail hesitated, considering Darby's expression. "You intrigue me."

"Well, you've hit the nail on the head. Congratulations. Seth has the hots for me, and I have the hots for him. We've both admitted it, but we're miles apart on everything else."

"Seriously?" came Katrina's voice.

Darby turned to find both Mandy and Katrina gaping at her. Oh, perfect. She might as well have blasted it over the airwaves.

"Wine, anyone?" she asked into the silence.

"Absolutely," said Mandy.

"Fruit juice," said Abigail with resignation.

Darby quickly headed back downstairs, darting into the kitchen and concentrating on selecting a bottle of merlot from her own wine rack.

What had she gone and done? How could she have been so careless?

"Seth's only ever dated casually," Mandy stated as she entered the kitchen behind Darby.

Darby peeled off the heavy foil and retrieved a corkscrew. "Seth and I are not dating."

"She might not want to talk about her sex life with his sisters," Katrina admonished. "This is a fantastic kitchen." She glanced around at the long counters, the new cabinets, a large stove and dual ovens. All were sparkling under the sunshine streaming through the big windows.

"Thanks." Darby popped the cork, grateful for an opportunity to change the topic, and more than willing to steer the conversation in a new direction. "The cook and the rest of the staff have the night off. But we normally feed ten to fifteen people."

"I really do think we should book a weekend here," said Mandy.

"That is a fantastic deck," noted Katrina. She'd moved to the bay window in the breakfast nook.

"It's very popular," Darby confirmed as she retrieved four wineglasses from a high shelf.

"I bet you drink wine out there," said Katrina.

"We do," Darby confirmed, crossing to the fridge and finding some juice for Abigail. "Passion-fruit–mango okay?" she called behind her.

"Compared to merlot? Absolutely not." Abigail gave a deep, exaggerated sigh. "But sacrifices must be made."

"Okay for us to drink out there?" Katrina asked brightly.

"Absolutely," said Darby. "It catches the afternoon sun, so it'll be warm for a while yet." She continued pouring the merlot.

"I heard you were in the military," said Mandy.

Darby nodded. "I'm still in the reserves."

"Our ranch was kind of like boot camp," Katrina mused. "Up at the crack of dawn, hard physical work, eating communally in the cook shack."

Mandy rolled her eyes. "You are such a princess."

Katrina grinned unrepentantly. "Reed likes it that way."

"Help yourself to a wineglass," Darby told them. "Down that little hall to the left will get us outside."

She took a glass for herself, handed the open bottle to Mandy then retrieved a second bottle of merlot for good measure. As she followed them out through the back door, she framed up a little speech on the peace and tranquility of Sierra Hotel. Nothing like a live demonstration to make her point.

They quickly settled themselves in the padded chairs. A few fluffy clouds marred the blue sky, and the lake was dead calm, reflecting the autumn-colored mountains on the far shore.

The sun streamed comfortably down on her body as she tried to come up with an opening line. Perhaps she could ask Abigail about the DFB restaurant, then segue into the ambiance and tranquility of Lyndon Valley.

"So why did you join the army?" Katrina asked Darby, setting her wineglass on a side table. She kicked off her sandals and wiggled her sparkling lavender-painted toes.

"Oh, that sun feels good," Abigail groaned.

"They paid for college," Darby answered Katrina. "It was just me and my mom, and she couldn't afford tuition, so it seemed like a good opportunity to get a degree."

She didn't mention that her mother thought college was a waste of time, and that she wouldn't have helped with tuition even if she had had any money.

"What's your degree in?" asked Abigail.

"Psychology."

"Mine's in history. But I should have taken business."

"You had to join the army to go to school?" Katrina seemed shocked. "I feel a little guilty here."

Mandy spoke up. "She was in private dance school in New York City from the time she was ten."

"It obviously paid off," said Darby. She knew Katrina was now a very successful dancer. "And don't feel sorry for me. The military was a good experience. I met some amazing women, and it's the reason I'm here today."

"What did your mom do?" asked Abigail.

"Cocktail waitress."

"And your dad?"

"Not a clue," said Darby, taking a swallow of her wine. "I expect he was married. Most of the customers who hit on my mom were married."

"It reminds me of Niki," said Katrina. "Reed and Caleb's newly discovered half sister," she added to Darby. "Their dad had a fling years ago in D.C."

"Without the wealth," Mandy put in. Again, obviously for Darby's benefit, she added, "Niki's mother, Gabriella, parlayed her sexual relationships into a very large Swiss bank account. She wanted to be sure Niki was secure."

"That's not at all like my mother," said Darby. "I think she expected me to follow in her footsteps. In a weird, very unhealthy way, she hated that I was more successful than her."

"What's your relationship like now?" asked Abigail.

Darby took another bracing drink. "We hadn't talked for a long time and then she passed away last year."

"I'm sorry," said Mandy.

"Families are tricky," Katrina added. "For most people, my upbringing would be a dream come true. But it was hell for me."

"Hell?" Mandy challenged.

"She was a delicate flower," said Abigail.

"I dreamed of toe shoes and tutus. I got cowboy boots and manure forks."

"I love ranching," said Mandy. "I've always loved ranching."

"What about you?" Darby turned the question to Abigail.

"I can live with ranching, but I like business better."

"You help run DFB?" Darby saw her chance to turn the conversation.

"Why did you leave the army?" Katrina asked.

Darby told herself to be patient. They had a whole bottle of wine to go. "My tour was up, and I thought I could help more in civilian life."

"Are you a psychologist now?" asked Abigail.

"Only to the extent that there's psychology in operating a women's retreat."

"She's also a bad-ass bodyguard," said Katrina. "We all heard about how you intimidated the pranksters."

"From Seth?" Darby couldn't help but ask.

"From Travis," said Mandy. "He heard it from a city council member. Seth stays away from gossip."

That was good to know, considering some of the things Darby had been doing with Seth.

"You look relieved," Abigail observed.

"No." Darby shook her head. "Just curious to know how information gets around in this town."

"Why do you hate the train so much?" Katrina asked.

Both of her sisters shot her a glare.

"What?" Katrina lifted her wineglass. "We're not allowed to mention the elephant on the deck?"

Darby couldn't help but smile. "Close your eyes," she told them all. "Listen."

She closed her own eyes, hearing the chirp of the birds, the rustle of the wind, the slight buzz of bumblebees and the faint gurgle of the wavelets on shore.

"Inhale deeply," she told them. "Now open your eyes. Take a look around."

The three women twisted their heads, taking in the meadows, the forest, the lake, the mountains and the blue sky.

"I don't want to lose this," Darby said softly. "I've stayed in hot, dusty deserts, ravaged by mortar shells and sandstorms, where the sky was blotted out by smoke in the day, or lit up by explosions and fires at night. You couldn't sleep more than an hour without being woken by gunfire or helicopters or the cries of the wounded. The water was polluted, and the air acrid."

She didn't add that many of Sierra Hotel's clients experienced exactly the same things, and far more recently than Darby. And they returned to it after their retreat. Others experienced the tension of inner-city gangs and the threat of harm or death on a daily basis.

"You were in combat?" Abigail asked.

"Mostly inside the wire," said Darby. "But I saw what combat did to others."

"Have you told Seth all this?" asked Mandy.

"Believe me, I've told Seth everything I can think of that might sway him."

"Hello?" came a man's voice in the distance, followed swiftly by footfalls around the corner of the house.

"That's our brother Travis," Abigail said.

"Girls' party back here," Mandy called from behind the latticework that partially concealed the deck.

The footsteps stopped. "Who's all here?"

"Hey, Travis," Abigail called.

"Abigail?"

"Yep. Me, Mandy and Katrina."

"I'm looking for Darby."

"She's here, too."

"I'm sorry to intrude, Darby," Travis said. "I brought someone up to see you. His name's Evan Parry, and his mother is a friend of mine. He wants to apologize to you for the other night."

Darby very much doubted Evan *wanted* to do anything of the sort. Still, she couldn't help but be impressed by Travis's actions. Evan should be made to stand up and explain. And it would be good to impress upon the kid just how dangerous and misguided his actions had been.

"I'll meet you in the great room," she called to Travis.

The gangly, thin-faced Evan was standing in the middle of her great room, shoulders stooped, head bent, longish hair partially covering his eyes. Travis stood behind him, arms folded across his chest, a grim expression on his face.

"Hello, Evan," Darby said.

The boy stayed silent.

Travis nudged him on the back of the shoulder.

"I'm here to say I'm sorry, ma'am."

"Look at her," said Travis.

Evan shot a brief glare at Travis, but then raised his chin to look at Darby.

"Again," Travis ordered.

"I'm sorry, ma'am," said Evan.

"Sorry for what?" she asked him levelly, not willing to let him off the hook too easily.

She saw a glint of admiration in Travis's eyes.

"I'm sorry we frightened you."

"You put us in real danger," Darby pointed out.

"We never—"

"Evan," Travis warned.

Evan swallowed. "I'm sorry if we put anybody in danger. And I'm sorry we trespassed. And I'm sorry we scared you."

"I don't believe you," said Darby.

Evan's pale blue eyes hardened in anger.

"It seems like you're saying what you think I want to hear."

"I'm sayin' what my mom told me I had to say."

"I don't want you to say you're sorry, Evan," said Darby. "I want you to understand what you did."

"I understand."

"No, you don't. You committed a crime. You shot a weapon. Somebody could have been hurt or killed. You could have been arrested and ended up with a criminal record. Try getting into college with that hanging over your head. And I don't know if anyone told you, but I fought in the army. If I'd had a weapon, if you'd pointed that gun at me, I could have shot you dead. You'd be dead, Evan. *Dead.* I want you to understand that."

Travis was looking at her with obvious amazement.

"And I would have shot and killed a sixteen-year-old boy for no good reason. You, dead. Me living with that mistake for the rest of my life. All because you made a colossal error in judgment. I want you to understand that."

"Yes, ma'am," Evan muttered, looking genuinely contrite for the first time.

"And I want to know what you're going to do differently next time. Next time you're drinking, or you get some asinine, testosterone-fueled idea in your head, or when one of your friends does it for you, I want to know how you're going to make a better decision."

Evan blinked in obvious confusion.

"Here's a hint," said Darby. "Think it through to the end, Evan. Think through every single thing that can go wrong, and where you'll end up when it does—in jail or in the ground. Because it will go wrong. It always goes wrong."

"It doesn't always—"

"Evan," Travis growled.

"It did this time," Darby said more softly. "And I'm willing to bet a whole lot of money you didn't expect it to go wrong."

"We didn't," Evan admitted.

"You're too old to behave like a child," she told him.

He was silent for a long moment, and she could see the debate going on inside his brain. His pride was battling reality.

"I'm sorry," he finally repeated.

"This time, I believe you. Thank you."

He nodded.

"Wait for me in the car," said Travis.

Evan didn't need a second invitation. He all but ran across the room and rushed outside, closing the door behind him.

"That was well-done," Travis told her, the look of amazement still there on his face.

"I hope it helps," she responded.

"How about you?" Travis asked. "You okay?"

"Okay how?"

If he meant had she recovered from the boys' prank, she was perfectly fine. It took a lot more than a couple of sixteen-year-olds to rattle her.

Travis nodded toward the kitchen and the back deck. "My sisters?"

"They stopped by. I'm giving them my side of the story," Darby said, seeing no reason to lie.

"Is it working?"

"I don't know yet."

He paused for a long moment. "Seth's worried about you," he said.

"So I've heard."

"But it seems to me that you're not afraid of much."

"I'm not afraid of Seth, if that's what you mean."

"It's more than that," said Travis. "And I've seen some of the women who come to stay here. They remind me of guys I know in the military, hard-core—"

"Thanks for stopping by, Travis." Darby moved toward the door, expecting him to follow.

"It makes me wonder," he mused as he did follow her, "with that kind of clientele, and given how oblique you are about this ladies' retreat, what's really going on up here?"

Darby smacked her hand onto the doorknob and rested it there. She thought through her next words. "Travis."

"Yeah?"

"It would be better if you didn't wonder."

He was silent for a long moment. "Would it be better if I didn't tell Seth?"

"It would be better if you didn't tell anyone."

He gave a crooked smile. "Our sisters. You've got guts, I'll grant you that."

Darby had made pastrami sandwiches on rye bread. She and the Jacobs sisters had laughed their way through the informal meal, and the lively conversation made her forget about co-opting them to her cause. They finished with chocolate cake before the three sisters headed back to town.

When Darby went out to pick up the glasses, she found half a bottle of wine was left. Dusk was falling, and the pot lights in the yard had automatically turned on. The lake and mountains were darkening, while cicadas came to life, and the wind whipped up the lake, pushing louder waves onto the sandy shore. She sighed, thinking Sierra Hotel was as close to heaven as humanly possible.

Thoughts of Seth and his family spinning through her mind, she opened up the big, whirlpool tub. Then she stripped off her clothes, poured some of the wine into a clean plastic glass from the outdoor cupboard and sank back into the warm water.

As she settled back, footsteps sounded on the wooden deck.

"Hello?" she called, wondering if one of the Jacobs sisters had forgotten something.

"It's Seth."

Heart tripping in her chest, she answered him. "Your sisters left. So did your brother."

"My sisters were here?" He came around the end of the screen.

"You didn't know?"

"I didn't know."

"They dropped by for a visit."

She knew the bubbling water kept her body hidden. But she was also acutely aware of the fact that she was naked.

"Why?" he asked, eyes narrowing.

"I think they were checking me out."

"They know we're fighting," he admitted.

"They also know we're attracted to each other."

"Well, I sure didn't tell them that."

"They're not stupid, Seth. They figured out that something was going on." And if they had figured it out, she couldn't help worrying that someone else might, as well.

"How much do they know?"

"I told them I had the hots for you."

His mouth flexed in a self-satisfied grin.

She ignored it. "I figured it was better to admit to that much than to let them guess anything else."

"You have the hots for me?"

"Had. Past tense," she lied.

His gaze slid meaningfully down to the roiling water that covered her nudity. "For me it's *have,* present tense."

Darby took refuge in a drink of wine, but it didn't do anything to quell her awareness of him.

"Travis called after he left here," he added.

Darby pulled up on her meandering hormones. She hoped Travis hadn't shared his suspicions about Sierra Hotel's military connection. She could understand his loyalty was to Seth and not to her, but gossip and speculation could be as bad for her future as the trains.

"Is that why you're here?" She probed, watching his expression, debating whether to come clean with him. It was a risk, admitting to anyone her true purpose at Berlynn Lake. But if Seth was already suspicious, wasn't it better to bring him onside? If she was very lucky, it might even help him understand the importance of her work.

"I came to give you this." He held up an envelope, looking uncomfortable enough to worry her.

"What is it?" she asked with suspicion. So much for confiding in him. Though at least she knew Travis was a man of his word.

"A check from the city."

She didn't reach for it.

"It's for the railway easement. The land appropriation went through."

Both his words and flat tone reminded her starkly that he was the enemy. It didn't matter how sexy he looked standing on her deck silhouetted by the mountains. She had no business wanting him. She had no business even considering wanting him all over again.

She put a hard edge into her tone. "So the city now owns part of my land."

"It was land you didn't even know you owned until two weeks ago."

"Don't I have to sign something to make it legal?"

He dropped the envelope on the side table. "The very nature of expropriation is that one party is unwilling. It would be ludicrous to expect you to sign."

"So that's that?"

"That's that." He paused, his expression softening enough to cause a little lurch in her chest. "I feel like I should apologize."

She valiantly fought the sensation. "Now *that* would be ludicrous."

"I am sorry." His apology seemed genuine, and she wished with all her heart she could separate Seth the man from Seth the mayor. But she didn't dare.

She stretched her arms across the lip of the hot tub. "At

the end of all this, one of us is going to lose big, Seth. And if I win the referendum, I'm not planning to apologize to you."

"Okay. Then I'm no longer sorry. At least, not about the expropriation."

She wanted to ask what he was sorry for, but she bit down on her tongue.

They stared at each other in the waning light, the hum of the whirlpool motor and the lap of the water a backdrop to the silent emotions thickening between them. She wanted him to go, but she also wanted him to stay. They were both adversaries and lovers, and there didn't seem to be a road map for that.

"Warm in there?" he asked.

"No."

He nodded, but stood silent, still, watchful, every inch the cowboy.

She lifted her wineglass, and he watched intently as she put it to her lips.

"Taste good?" he asked in a deep, stirring voice.

"No."

"You're not going to make this easy, are you?"

"I'm never going to make anything easy ever again."

His mouth quirked in a half smile. "I'm pretty much counting on that." Still, he didn't leave, just stood there watching her while the warm water burbled around her bare thighs, teasing her skin, arousing her senses.

She cracked. "There's an extra wineglass on the table."

"Yeah?" He didn't move.

She cast her gaze to the foaming water, then looked back up. "That's as easy as I'm going to make it, Seth."

Eight

Glass of merlot in one hand, Seth eased his body into the warm water of Darby's large whirlpool tub. Sitting on the opposite side, she was gorgeous as always. Water foamed around her bare shoulders, dampening her auburn hair, while the filtered glow of the porch light silhouetted her face against the backdrop of dark hills. He sipped his wine, not making any further assumptions on her meaning, content to stay quiet and watch her.

She didn't seem bothered by the silence, gazing right back at him.

"You met with my sisters?" He opened with something relatively safe. And he couldn't help wondering how that had come about.

"They wanted to see the place," she answered.

"Are you trying to recruit them?"

"I am," she admitted openly. "Then, I'm hoping they can influence you."

He smiled at her easy admission. He liked the way she hadn't evaded, pulled punches or danced around the issue.

"Is it working?" He stretched one arm across the edge of the tub.

"I'm not sure. They're talking about coming back here for a weekend getaway."

"You're bribing them?"

"I got the impression they planned to pay. I didn't offer a freebie." She toyed with the stem of her wineglass. "Though, now that you mention it..."

"You can't use my own ideas against me."

"Sure I can. All's fair in...whatever this is."

"What is this, Darby?" He sure couldn't figure it out.

"A flirtation?" she suggested. "A fight?"

"I don't want to fight with you," he told her honestly. "I do want to flirt with you."

"Only because it helps with your fight."

"I wish it was that simple."

"Then let's make it simple."

"And how do we do that?"

"We either stop flirting or we stop fighting." As she spoke, the underwater lights came on, giving him an indistinct view of creamy skin beneath the surface. He was momentarily speechless.

"Photo sensor," she explained. "They're automatic."

Seth didn't quite manage a reply.

He took a swig of the wine, telling himself to get a grip. She was naked, and she was beautiful.

"Travis seems to be doing okay." She shifted the conversation. "That was a smart thing he did, bringing Evan up here."

Seth didn't want to stop flirting. "Travis is a smart guy."

"So no danger of him getting in another fistfight?"

"In the theoretical, my brother knows what to do and what not to do. But he's got a temper, and if he thinks someone close to him needs defending, he'll defend them."

"That someone being you?"

"The family, our business interests or more generally the interests of the entire ranching community."

"That's a lot of people to defend."

"So I'm a little worried."

Darby unexpectedly smiled, and it lit up her face. Her green eyes glowed in the dim light, and the steam rising from the tub gave her an angelic appearance.

"Do you like having a big family?" she asked.

The question surprised him, but he rolled with it. He could handle a long game when necessary. "I do. And temper notwithstanding, Travis is a great brother."

"Your sisters seem very nice."

"For the most part, we all get along. My father had a stroke a couple of years ago, and my parents moved to Palm Springs after his rehab. But we see them as often as we can."

"It's hard to imagine," said Darby, swirling the tip of her index finger in a figure-eight pattern through the surface of the water.

Seth tried not to let the action turn him on. Trouble was, when she breathed it turned him on.

"Mom," she continued, "dad, siblings. You probably have a white picket fence and a dog."

"Lots of white picket fences and quite a few dogs."

"Tell me."

"Tell you what?"

"About your family. About a typical day with them, or even a typical dinner. What was dinner like?"

"My mom loved to cook," said Seth, realizing he was content to sit here talking with Darby. They weren't arguing, and that had to be progress. "She baked amazing pies and cakes and cookies."

"You're making me hungry."

"We had, well, still have, this huge, rectangular table in the dining room. Mom would empty the oven, clear off the stove, then pass all the dishes across the counter to the table. And then, look out."

"Look out?"

"We were usually all starving from working on the ranch all day long. Food disappeared pretty quickly."

"What did she cook?"

"Roast beef, potatoes, carrots, beans, ham, apple pie. All the staples. We had a barbecue out back for burgers and hot dogs, but I don't recall her grilling steaks when Travis and I were teenagers. I think she went for volume. Now we go for flavor."

"My mom was a fan of the microwave. Preformed, pre-packaged, precooked."

"Are you trying to make me pity you?"

"I am." She grinned into her wineglass before taking another drink. "Of course, I was well prepared for army food. I couldn't figure out what all the complaints were about."

"I'm going to have to bring you home for a proper dinner."

As soon as the words were out, he realized what he'd said. Was he suggesting he bring Darby home to his family? He couldn't bring Darby home to his family. Could he?

"You look like you just swallowed a spider," she observed. "Don't worry, Seth. I'm not going to hold you to that invitation."

That wasn't what he was thinking. Not at all. In fact, he was surprised to realize he *did* want to bring her home to his family. How had that happened? He'd gone from fighting with her to sleeping with her, and now he wanted to show her off to his sisters and brother?

"Whatever you're thinking," Darby broke in, "you should stop."

"I was thinking I'd like more wine," he said, draining his glass.

She glanced to the empty bottle. "Wine rack's in the kitchen."

"Corkscrew?"

"On the counter."

"Anybody else home?"

"Just you and me. But there are robes in the white cupboard."

"As long as it's just you and me." He rose out of the water, stepping onto the cedar deck.

While opening the wine, he decided to give his worries a rest. There were a million unsettling things occupying space in his brain, a million reasons to leave right now, a million reasons to stay the hell away from Darby. There was only one reason to climb back into the whirlpool tub.

He wanted to. It was as simple as that. He wanted to be here with her right now, and everything else could damn well wait until tomorrow.

He returned to the deck, topped up her glass, refilled his own and settled back into the water.

"Did you date in the military?" he asked.

There was a lingering suspicion in her green eyes, but she answered him, anyway. "Sometimes, depending on where I was stationed."

"Anything serious?"

"As it turned out, no."

He was intrigued. "But you thought it might be serious?"

"More like, he hoped I wouldn't notice he had a wife back in the States. But his buddies gave him up." She took a drink. "And he was a nice guy, too. You know, other than the little problem with fidelity."

"I'm in favor of fidelity," said Seth.

"Everyone *says* they're in favor of fidelity."

"My mama beat a few principles into me. I'd never cheat. I don't have a girlfriend now. In case you're wondering."

Darby gave a little laugh. "Are you defending not cheating on her?"

"There is no her." He covered his expression with a sip of his wine. "What about you?"

"Unattached."

A wave of relief loosened muscles Seth didn't even know he'd clenched.

"That's good," he told her.

"Would you have been disappointed in me if I'd cheated?" she asked in a teasing tone.

He would have been. It was a little frightening to realize how upset he would have been to discover there was another man in her life. He had a sudden, overwhelming urge to hold her in his arms, maybe trap her there, keep her away from anyone else.

He set down his wineglass. "Come here."

Her green eyes widened.

"Over here." He crooked his finger.

"You want to flirt some more, don't you?"

"I sure don't want to fight."

She hesitated. "You know what's going to happen if I come over there."

He wasn't about to deny it. "I need to touch you," he told her gruffly. "I need to hold you."

He waited, letting her make up her mind.

After a long moment, she squared her shoulders, rising, glass in hand. Droplets of water rolled down her shoulders, across her breasts. Steam clung to her upswept hair, giving her face a dewy glow.

Halfway, she stumbled, and he reached for her, grasping her hand and guiding her into his lap. She felt incredibly good against him, her warm, slippery skin, soft curves, the way her bottom fit across his thighs.

"Exactly how much have you had to drink?" he whispered into her ear.

"A couple of glasses," she sighed. "A few, I guess."

"Intoxicated?"

"A little."

Seth swallowed his disappointment. If her judgment was impaired, there was no way he could make love with her right now. But, unable to resist, he set aside their glasses and captured her moist mouth in a deep, lingering kiss.

He let it go on as long as he dared, but then forced himself to pull back. His point of no return was a hair trigger when it came to Darby. He settled her head against his shoulder, loosening his hold around her.

"Seriously?" she asked him in obvious surprise.

"You've been drinking," he told her.

"And you're going to be a gentleman about it?"

"I am."

"Wow."

"Don't sound so surprised." He shifted beneath her, settling them more comfortably, willing his body to back off its arousal. "It makes me worry about what you think of me."

"I think I don't know you very well. This old-fashioned sense of chivalry is a surprise."

"I guess that makes us even. Because you surprise me over and over again."

Darby awoke in Seth's arms. He'd put off making love to her last night, but they'd ended up in her bed, anyway, cuddled together in white Sierra Hotel bathrobes, where she'd fallen asleep feeling warm and protected.

It was still full dark, probably somewhere around three. The wind had come up in the night. The flag was snapping on its pole, while the waves echoed on the lakeshore. Something fell outside, crashing hard on what she guessed was the back patio.

"What's that?" Seth came awake, stiffening beside her.

"The wind," she replied, curling against his warm body. It had been close to paradise, merely being held in his arms earlier. And there was no reason for them to stop now.

She liked the sound of the wind. It reminded her that she was at Berlynn Lake instead of in a basement suite in the inner city.

Something clattered across the deck, banging into the kitchen wall.

Seth sat up. "Is someone out there?"

"It's the wind blowing things around."

He swung his legs over the side of the bed. "We don't know that for sure."

"Listen to the waves."

He paused to listen.

The waves were clear to hear, but so were other sounds, creaking and scraping, and something made of glass shattered.

"An empty wine bottle," Darby guessed.

"I'm going to check it out."

"We'll get it in the morning." She didn't want him to leave right now. She wasn't sure she ever wanted him to leave.

But he came to his feet. "If somebody's out there—"

"There's nobody out there." Darby came up on the backs of her elbows. "And if there is, you want them to see you? Here? In the middle of the night? Fraternizing with the enemy?"

"Better than having them light your inn on fire."

"If we smell smoke, we'll go outside. *I'll* go outside."

He gave a sarcastic laugh. "Yeah, right."

She reached out and touched his robe-covered thigh, wanting to recapture a softer mood. "We can't let anyone see you here, Seth."

"So you admit somebody's out there."

"I admit nothing." She stroked her hand along the terry cloth, coming to the edge of the robe and encountering bare skin. "You should come back to bed."

He went still.

"I'm completely sober now," she whispered into the dark.

There was another clattering sound on the deck and his muscles stiffened.

"Beach chair," she whispered reassuringly, listening closely to the array of sounds. "Flag. Waves. Hot tub cover. And a tree branch."

She feathered her fingertips along his skin.

"You are ridiculously distracting." His voice was tight.

"Come back to bed and fraternize." She parted his robe and kissed his bare thigh.

He dropped to the bed. His arm snaked around her waist, pulling her rear out from under her, pressing her back into the soft mattress. "If the place burns down, it's all your fault."

"The only thing on fire here is me." She wrapped her arms around his neck.

It felt so good to have him in her bed. It felt right, easy, as easy as drawing her next breath.

"And me," he rasped, capturing her mouth in a deep kiss.

She pushed his bathrobe off his shoulders. "Good to hear."

He reached between them, tugged at her sash and splayed her robe open, too. "You are exquisitely beautiful."

She swirled her fingertips along his bare chest, down his hard abs, farther, until she wrapped her hand around his heat.

A growl rumbled through his chest, and he instantly came down on top of her. His mouth opened, fusing with hers in the heated kiss, his tongue calling to hers, his hands gripping her hips.

Her back arched, her legs separating, while his hand slipped between. She was slick, and he was obviously hungry.

"You are so hot," he rasped. "So unbelievably sweet."

Her mind blanked out everything but Seth. She hugged him tight, kissed him frantically, guided him mindlessly toward her. There was no time to waste, no time for anything but completion.

"Condom," he whispered, holding back.

"It's fine. I use birth control." The hormone shots were a convenience thing in the military, but right now it meant nothing but Seth.

"You're amazing." His mouth captured hers. His hips flexed forward, and he buried himself deep.

"That's good," she moaned. "Good, good, good."

She wrapped her arms around him, while his moved beneath her, holding her tight.

He turned onto his back. She straddled him, pressed tight, shocks of sensation exploding through her body. He moved, and she answered. His hands went to her breasts, strumming over her nipples, adding to the cacophony of sensations bombarding her brain.

She leaned over him, bracing herself, kissing his chest, his neck, his hot, moist mouth. Their bodies slammed together, harder and faster, lights swirling behind her eyes. Time sped up, then stopped, as she hovered on the precipice of ecstasy.

Then Seth shouted her name, and the world roared down around her. Her muscles contracted, and she collapsed onto his chest. His arms went immediately around her, and he groaned her name over and over in her ear.

Darby wanted to make a joke, or a flip comment—something to keep her intense emotions at bay. But she couldn't find any words. She couldn't form a single thought except that she'd never felt like this before. She wanted to hang on tight to Seth and pretend the rest of the world didn't exist.

So she did.

Just for a few moments.

She squeezed her eyes shut, reveled in his warm, slick skin next to hers, inhaled his spicy scent and let her breathing and heart rate sync up with his.

He stroked his palm along the back of her head, smoothing her riotous hair. He wordlessly gathered her close, his forearm across the small of her back, keeping their bodies fused.

His breathing gradually slowed down. His heart steadied in his chest. And he pulled her quilt over both of them, enveloping them together in a warm cocoon.

Warm against him, she felt consciousness slip away. She was weightless, riding waves of smooth, random thoughts that took her from her bed to a warm pool, to a sunny beach.

"Sometimes you frighten me." He broke huskily into her meandering brain waves. "If this is a secret plot to control me, I think you just succeeded."

"It's not a secret," she managed to echo back on an exhale. "I told you that's been my mission all along."

"You are a dangerous woman, Darby Carroll."

"Give up, Seth Jacobs. Give in, and do things my way."

"This is a bad time for me to make that decision."

She found herself smiling. "It's the perfect time for you to make that decision."

Instead of answering, he gathered her more closely in his arms, kissing her softly and cradling her against the warmth and strength of his body.

In the morning, Seth expected to find Darby in the kitchen, but he was shocked to find Lisa there, as well.

"Morning?" he ventured, wondering what Lisa could possibly be doing at Sierra Hotel.

"Mayor," said Lisa, her tone crisp as she stood up from the breakfast bar where she'd been drinking coffee. "We need you back at City Hall."

Darby handed Seth a stoneware mug of hot coffee.

"You couldn't have called my cell?" Seth took a reflexive sip of the beverage, appreciating the hit of caffeine. Maybe if his brain was functioning, this would start to make sense.

"I've been trying since six a.m. You turn it off?"

"No." Seth extracted the phone from his inner-suit-jacket pocket. "Battery's dead."

"Rather than have people mount a full-blown search party, I thought I better track you down. It was Abigail who guessed where to look."

"I'd have come in on time." Seth wasn't sure whether to thank her for being discreet or to strongly suggest she and his sisters mind their own damn business.

"We need you right away. I'll explain in the car."

Darby had parked herself against a counter, her expression neutral. He hoped she hadn't confessed anything to Lisa.

"I drank too much wine last night," Seth told Lisa easily. "Stayed over. It's a hotel."

Lisa's lifted eyebrow suggested that she challenged the story, and she glanced at Darby. But Darby didn't flinch.

"I'll meet you in the car," Seth told Lisa.

"We need to go *now*," she reiterated, but she moved toward the great room.

Seth crossed to Darby. "I'm sorry."

"Don't worry about it."

"She doesn't know anything."

"She knows everything."

Seth paused, working up an argument. But there was really no point. Darby was right and they both knew it.

He sighed in resignation. "She's discreet."

"It's was a mistake for you to stay."

"No." He shook his head. "It's a mistake for me to go."

"Seth, it's time for you to go."

Her calm conviction gave him pause. Most women would be upset by such an abrupt departure. Things had changed for him last night. Had they not changed for her?

"I thought we could at least have breakfast together."

"I understand you're a very busy man."

He searched for a trace of sarcasm, but couldn't find any. "What do you mean by that?"

She cocked her head sideways. "Let me see. I mean you're a busy man, and I'm aware of that fact."

"Are you upset?" he couldn't help but ask.

"Are you feeling guilty?"

"About leaving, yes. But not about anything else." He didn't regret a single moment they'd spent together. His sisters could speculate, and Lisa would have to be discreet. He'd date Darby openly if he could. He'd love nothing better than to date her.

"Good. Then go with Lisa. Get back to your regularly scheduled life, and don't worry about me."

"We gotta go," Lisa called from the front door.

"Be right there," Seth called over his shoulder. "You sure you're okay?" he repeated to Darby.

"Perfect," said Darby.

Unsatisfied, but unable to think of anything else to do, he turned for the door.

"Let's take your car," said Lisa. "I can come back later for mine."

"What's going on?" Seth asked as he fished his car keys from the pocket of his slacks.

It was nearly 8:00 a.m. The sun was up, temperature rising as they headed into another clear, fall day.

"Clive Loring called this morning," Lisa began. "He's in town and wants to meet with you."

Seth paused with his hand on the driver's door handle. Clive Loring was the president of Western Railroad, and he didn't tend to show up when things were going well.

"Do you know why he's here?" Seth asked.

"We're trying to find out, but he insists on seeing you right away."

Lisa's phone chimed. She pulled it out as she climbed into the car.

Seth got in and turned the key, his mind going through possible scenarios. Had Clive heard about the escalating feud in Lyndon? Was he worried about the negative publicity for Mountain Railway? Was he getting impatient? Was he unwilling to wait through the referendum time period?

"Uh-oh," said Lisa, as she read the text on her phone.

"What?" asked Seth, swinging the car around and heading down the gravel road.

"I've got some new information. Wadesworth County has submitted a counter-proposal. They want the railroad to parallel Jimmydee Road."

"How'd they pull that off so fast?"

Lyndon City had been working on their final proposal for months. Years, if you counted all the preliminary work.

"Looks like they've quietly been at it for a while now. Their permitting is already in place."

Seth frowned. "Waiting in the wings, just looking for an opportunity to pounce."

"Arguably, both lines could eventually be constructed," said Lisa.

"Mountain Railway only needs one shorter link to Ripple Ridge."

Darby hadn't been wrong about that being the obvious long-term plan.

Seth stepped more firmly on the accelerator. "If they get it through Wadesworth, our project is mothballed indefinitely."

"There's more than a month left until the referendum."

"Call Mandy," Seth told Lisa.

"You think Mandy can help?"

"Tell her we need Danielle Marin to fly in."

"Caleb's lawyer?"

"Caleb's laywer," said Seth. "She's a tactical genius."

Lisa looked doubtful. "You think a Chicago lawyer is going to help us in Colorado?"

"We're running out of options. If we don't do something quick, Darby won't need to win the referendum. We'll lose the railroad by the end of the week."

Nine

Marta arrived shortly after Seth left. She'd brought several packages from the post office. After lugging them inside, the women blended some fruit-and-yogurt smoothies and sat down at the breakfast bar.

"Seth spent the night," Darby began bluntly, bracing her feet on the crossbar of the high chair.

Marta's spoon came to a halt midscoop. "Say what?"

"He came by yesterday. We had some wine. It got late, and he ended up staying."

"Do you mean staying, or *staying?*"

"He slept in my bed."

"Just to be completely clear before I react to this, you slept there, too?"

Darby laughed, wheezing as she inhaled some of the fruit smoothie. "I wasn't trying to be oblique."

"I was all for flirting, but this… Wow, you're putting your heart and soul into distracting the man."

Darby drew a heavy sigh. "He's doing a pretty good job of

distracting me, too. He's not what I expected, Mar. He's more complicated. He's actually a pretty decent guy."

"You mean, aside from the fact that his railroad will ruin your business?"

"Right. If you were to take that little flaw away…"

Marta arched a brow.

Darby realized she'd give a lot to take that one little flaw away.

"A little flaw can be a big flaw," said Marta. "You need to be careful. You don't want to lose Sierra Hotel and your heart in one fell swoop."

"I don't think—" Darby stopped. She was sure her heart wasn't at risk. At least she was pretty sure. Okay, she'd *make* sure her heart wasn't at risk.

She regrouped. "I don't mind losing in a fair fight." At least she didn't think she'd mind. Maybe "mind" wasn't the best word. "I could *live* with losing in a fair fight," she amended.

"Could you live with Seth after he won the fair fight?"

"Are we getting ahead of ourselves? I slept with the man. I didn't offer to have his children."

"Only once?" Marta asked, watching her closely.

"Twice. Well, it depends on how you count. But on two separate occasions."

"But your heart's okay?" Marta asked skeptically.

"I like him. But it's nothing past that. He showed up last night to give me a check. On another topic entirely, expropriation went through."

"Unfortunately, that was inevitable. But I'm not seeing a straight line from that to sleeping with him."

"It wasn't a straight line. It's never been a straight line with Seth. It was a strange day all around. First I visited with his sisters, all three of them. They're pretty nice, too."

"Are you losing your appetite for the fight?"

"No. No," Darby repeated with determination. "If I lose the fight, we lose Sierra Hotel, and some of the greatest women in America lose an important emotional support system."

"Agreed," said Marta. "So what are you going to do next?"

"I don't want to lose my edge."

"Then stay out of Seth's bed."

Darby reluctantly agreed. "And I don't want any more vandalism or bar fights."

Marta came to her feet, taking her empty glass to the sink and filling it with water. "I've been thinking about this."

"Good."

"And I've come up with another idea."

"I'm all ears."

"There are two tacks you can take here. You can make it harder for him to win, or you can make it easier for him to lose."

Darby followed suit, rinsing her own glass and placing it in the dishwasher. "I'm not sure I follow."

"Up to now, we've been pointing out the dangers of the railway, how Lyndon will be negatively impacted if it's built. What if we do a one-eighty? We gather some information on shipping alternatives for the ranchers. What trucking companies are out there that they might not have used in the past. Could a local company be set up, maybe even a co-op that could offer shipping at a reduced rate?"

"We give the other side a path forward." Darby nodded.

"Giving someone a workable and dignified exit is often a good strategy, especially if you've developed feelings for them."

"I can cope with my feelings," Darby assured her, determined that it would remain true.

"I don't think either of us sees a win-win here," said Marta. "But maybe we can pull off a win–not-so-ugly lose."

"We need to take them out of the game before they even know what hit them," Danielle Marin said. She was seated in the Jacobses' ranch house living room. "We can't waste a few more weeks waiting on the referendum."

She'd flown straight into Lyndon on Caleb's jet. Having

obviously studied the issue in flight, she now sat with Caleb, Mandy and Seth, strategizing their next move.

Seth was all for making this swift and decisive. His council members agreed; they couldn't afford to let Wadesworth County get a toehold on the project.

"Any ideas on how?" he asked.

"Your judgment to grant the referendum is from a district court," said Danielle. "We appeal the decision to the state. From what I can see, there was no point in law for granting the referendum."

"Then why did they get it?" asked Seth.

"The final few signatures were definitely late. We can argue the judge made an error in letting the referendum go ahead on the basis of 'what was good for Lyndon City.'"

"It was the judge's opinion only. That's always shaky ground."

"Darby will fight at the state level," said Seth. He had no reason to believe she'd back down from that.

"She can't," said Danielle. "She may be a party to the matter of the late signatures on the petition. But she's not technically a party to the matter of the referendum being 'in the public interest.' The wording of the judge's ruling leaves her out."

"So we can fight it without telling her?" asked Caleb.

"She has no legal right to know," Danielle clarified.

"I liked Darby," Mandy put in.

Seth found himself shifting in his chair. He liked Darby, too, but that didn't change his obligations as mayor. He couldn't sacrifice the good of his city to make a woman happy.

The front door swung open, and Travis appeared.

"What's all this—" He stopped, his gaze coming to an abrupt halt on Danielle.

"Hello, Travis," Danielle said.

Travis's body stiffened. "I didn't know you were here."

Since Travis had rescued Danielle from an embarrassing

escapade with a barn and a bull, the two had been oil and
water. But there wasn't time to indulge in their little feud now.

"How fast can you get a decision at the state level?" Seth
asked Danielle.

She pulled her attention back to Seth. "I can leave for
Denver tonight."

"How confident are you?" asked Caleb.

"Ninety-nine percent," said Danielle. "I'd give it a hundred, but lightning might strike the courthouse before I can
get there."

"Do it," said Seth, forcing Darby from his mind.

"Mandy and I'll drop you off in Denver," Caleb offered,
rising. "I need to get back to Chicago."

Mandy came to her feet, looking closely at Seth. "Damn
the torpedoes?"

He wasn't sure he got her point.

Taking in his expression, she clarified. "You're throwing
Darby under the bus."

"Darby always knew the score." He felt like a heel utter-
ing the words. But they were true. He might like her, but he'd
never promised to back off from the fight.

Mandy stopped beside him, speaking in a lower tone. "So
nothing's changed?"

He peered at her quizzically. "Why would anything have
changed?"

"She told me you found her attractive."

Seth wished he dared ask about the rest of that conversation, about Darby's feelings for him. But he wasn't about to
do that now, maybe not ever.

"She's a beautiful woman," he allowed.

"Are you sending her mixed signals?" his sister demanded.

"No."

He honestly wasn't sure if he was lying about that. Was
sleeping with her a mixed signal? Was letting her know she
was getting under his skin a mixed signal?

"You're going behind her back on this," Mandy said.

"She knows I'm out to win."

"Maybe so. But if you've given her reason to believe you care about her…"

He hadn't. It wasn't like either of them had kept their priorities a secret. Hell, she'd made jokes about sleeping with him in order to distract him from their fight. She wasn't about to turn into a wounded deer because he'd found another avenue to fight her, he was sure. She was tougher than that.

"Don't worry about Darby," he told Mandy.

She gave him a pitying smile. "I'm not worried about Darby."

He raised his brows in a question.

She gave him a pointed glare. "I'm worried about you."

"Ready to go?" Caleb asked his wife.

"Ready to go," Mandy confirmed.

As Danielle passed Travis on the way to the door, Seth heard him mutter, "Pretty cocky in your confidence."

She paused without looking at him. "You wrangle the bulls. I'll wrangle the judges."

Travis leaned in and whispered something in her ear.

Her lips flattened out, and a blush rose on her cheeks.

What the hell was the matter with his little brother? Didn't he know the woman was helping them?

"In your dreams," muttered Danielle. "And in my nightmares."

"Good luck," Travis told her out loud.

She turned her head to meet his gaze, and Seth watched his brother give her an insultingly insolent once-over. Then his lips curved into a cocky smile. As he watched her walk away, lust was all but naked in his expression.

The door closed behind them.

"What is wrong with you?" Seth asked.

Travis blinked at him. "What?"

"Danielle is *helping* us. She's *doing us a favor.*"

Travis dropped into an armchair. "If you want a shark on your team, she's the one to call in, all right."

"What is your problem with her?"

"You mean my problem with the uptight city chick who won't give the dusty cowboy the time of day no matter how many favors he does her?"

Seth pointed at his brother. "Put your libido on hold, and check your ego at the door, and let the nice lady lawyer help us out here."

"I hauled her sorry ass halfway across the Eldridges' field, and she didn't even have the grace to say thank you."

"Get over it."

Travis slumped back in his chair, the fight seeming to go out of him. "She'll do a good job for you, Seth. She's laser-focused that way."

Seth dropped into another chair. "How would you know that?"

"From Caleb. From her. I've heard what she says, and I've seen what she does."

"And you're so into her, you can't see straight."

"It's better when she's not around," Travis admitted. Then he gave a self-deprecating laugh. "Did you get a *look* at her?"

"She's pretty," Seth admitted. Not that he was remotely attracted to her. Which was odd, when he thought about it.

Maybe he'd been too focused on Danielle's role as a lawyer to think about her in any other way. Or maybe he'd been so completely satisfied by Darby last night that he didn't want sex today.

Well, except with Darby. If Darby was here, sex would be all Seth was thinking about.

"Seth?" Travis's hard voice interrupted his thoughts.

"Hmm?"

"You better not be thinking about Danielle."

Seth blinked his brother back into focus. "I'm not thinking about Danielle."

"Good."

No. Not good. It was fine to have a thing for Darby because she was a beautiful, sexy woman. But if it went beyond that, Mandy was right: he was going to get himself into a whole lot of trouble.

Darby tacked the new poster on the bulletin board in the foyer of City Hall. Captioned "Jobs for Lyndon Valley," it was bright, friendly and positive. Children frolicked in the background on a wildflower-strewn meadow, while a rugged, working-class man gazed with satisfaction at his shiny new transport truck. Smaller print listed the economic benefits of developing local transportation options, including a trucking co-op.

It was late afternoon, and Darby had been putting the posters up all around town. They'd revamped the website, and they were working on a few new radio spots.

"New tactic?"

Seth was right behind her.

"I don't think it'll incite any bar fights," she responded, pushing in the bottom tacks.

It had been three days since she'd seen him and made love with him. Still, the mere sound of his voice had the power to send tingles skipping along her nervous system. She wasn't sure what would happen if she turned to look at him.

"Interesting." He was obviously reading over her shoulder. "A trucking co-op?"

"Keep the jobs local," she responded. Then she drew a bracing breath and turned. "Who wouldn't be in favor of keeping the jobs local?"

"Kind of like apple pie and motherhood." His deep blue gaze bore into hers.

"Perennial favorites," she responded.

"How are you doing?" he asked in a lower tone.

"I'm fine." She didn't want to talk about anything that alluded to their night at her place, definitely not while standing in a public lobby. "Is the citizen discord staying under control?"

"A few public arguments and some letters to the editor, but nothing serious."

"Good night, Mr. Mayor," called a cheerful, female voice from across the foyer.

"Good night, Sally," Seth responded over his shoulder. "Good luck to the boys."

A thirtysomething woman gave a wave in response.

"My receptionist," he explained to Darby. "Her six-year-old twins have a baseball game tonight."

"Your staff seems to like you," Darby observed.

As she had at the Rodeo Association dinner, she couldn't help but notice how positively the city workers seemed to react to Seth.

"They're a great bunch of people."

Several more called and waved on their way out the door.

Darby knew she should say goodbye, as well. She hadn't expected to see Seth here. Okay, maybe half of her had hoped she would, but the other half had definitely hoped she wouldn't.

Her physical attraction to him was strong as ever, stronger, if that was possible, and it remained a colossally bad idea.

"I've missed you," he told her quietly.

"You can't do that," she responded, equally quietly.

"I mean talking to you, debating with you. Life's a little dull when you're not around."

"We can't be seen together," she told him.

"We can if it's official business."

"What official business do we have, other than fighting?"

"Persuasion. I need to persuade you to join my side."

"You've tried."

"Have you ever seen the art gallery?"

"Excuse me?"

"City Hall has an official art gallery. All citizens are welcome. I'm thinking it might help you understand our roots, the importance of a strong ranching community in the Valley. Now that I think about it, I realize it's vital for the cause that you take a look."

"An art gallery isn't going to change my mind, Seth."

"You don't know that until you've seen it."

"Isn't it closed?" she asked, taking note of the steady stream of staff exiting the building.

"Not yet. Besides, I have the keys."

Would it hurt to tour the art gallery with Seth? Neither of them would change the other's mind. And it would give them a few more minutes together. She'd missed him. She hadn't realized until that very moment just how much.

He cocked his head. "This way."

Giving in, Darby slung her bag over her shoulder and fell into step beside him.

"It's mostly oil paintings," he explained in a loud voice as they crossed the reception area. "But some of them date back to the 1700s. I'm sure you'll find them compelling."

"I'll look at them," she responded for the benefit of the people moving through the lobby. "But you won't change my mind."

"There's one of my great-great-grandfather's original homestead," Seth continued. "Back then, the ranching community worked incredibly hard. It was a tiny house. I can't even imagine how they lasted through the winter with four boys."

They left the lobby, taking a small marble staircase with polished brass railings to a short hallway half a story down.

"Is the house still there?" she found herself asking, feeling oddly curious about his ancestors.

"The potbellied stove, the chimney and a bit of the foundation. Mandy thinks we should restore it."

"You should." Darby agreed with Mandy.

She couldn't even imagine having that kind of family history at her fingertips. Her mother hadn't owned real estate. And she was pretty sure her grandparents had never put down roots. The only thing her mother ever said about them was that Darby's grandfather was a drunk of a salesman, and her grandmother should have known better than to marry him.

They'd had one small photo album in the apartment, and it contained a few pictures of her grandparents around a spindly Christmas tree. That was all Darby knew of them.

Seth pulled open a glass door, and lights automatically came up in the gallery.

It appeared to be a series of small, connected rooms, compact but immaculate, with cream-colored walls, polished, pine benches and diffuse spotlights on each of the paintings.

"It goes in approximate historical order," he explained, pointing to one of the walls.

"I see a theme here," she noted, moving slowly along the oil paintings of fields, log cabins, mountains and cattle.

She quickly found herself absorbed by the early lives of the settlers. Making her way from painting to painting, she stopped to gaze at some beautiful horse portraits.

"Madeline Parker," said Seth, his voice low. "She was born in the Valley in 1901. Extraordinarily talented. Her paintings have become quite valuable. There's even one hanging in a museum in Houston."

"Did she paint anything besides horses?"

He turned and indicated the wall behind them. "We have one of her landscapes."

Darby moved, positioning herself five feet from the scene of flowers and mountains. The painting showed a small, aging house in the background and three horses in the distance.

"It's breathtaking."

Seth motioned to the picture next to it. "This one is my great-great-grandparents' house."

Darby gazed at it for a long moment, easily imagining a close-knit family moving around the little house, laughing, eating, sleeping, working. She turned to look at Seth's profile. "So that was the original Jacobs ranch?"

"Yes. It's higher up in the hills than the main compound now, so it looks quite different."

"You should live up there," said Darby, turning back to the painting. "Seriously, Seth. If I were you, I'd turn that old foundation into a brand-new house."

"You think?"

"Mandy's onto something. I think your great-great-grandparents would definitely like that."

"You know this how?" he asked indulgently.

"Because, if I was anybody's great-great-grandparent I'd be thrilled to know they lived in the same place I had lived." She paused. "Well, of course, I don't mean in that crappy, basement apartment. Nobody's grandchildren should be forced to live there. I mean, if I had a beautiful homestead on a gorgeous piece of property, I'd love it if it carried on through the generations."

Seth didn't respond, and she let her gaze linger on the painting for a long time before moving around the corner to the next gallery.

It took nearly an hour for them to make it through, ending up with the newest oil paintings of Lyndon City and the rodeo fairgrounds.

"What's through there?" she asked, pointing to a narrow stone archway with a velvet rope across it.

"Want to see?" he asked on a definite note of mischief.

"Are we allowed?"

He unhooked the velvet rope. "You really aren't getting the part where I'm in charge here, are you?"

"That doesn't mean we should break the rules."

He gestured for her to go first. "Seriously? You're that straight-laced?"

She started down the passage. "You think I'm straight-laced?"

"I didn't. Not until now."

"Well, I'm not." She gave her hair a little toss. "I can be quite the maverick."

He choked out a laugh, as a metal door loomed up in front of them.

"What?" she demanded. "You don't believe me?"

"It's not that."

"What is it?"

"I was going to make a roping and riding joke, but that would be completely inappropriate."

What was completely inappropriate was Darby's reaction to his words. Arousal shunted through her body, bringing a rush of heat to her skin.

"You asked," he intoned behind her.

She reached for the doorknob.

"It's locked," said Seth, reaching into his pocket, fishing out a key.

She stepped aside.

"I'm sorry," he told her as he inserted it into the lock. "I shouldn't be so crude."

"No need." She struggled to keep her voice neutral. "I'm sure it would have been a very funny joke."

He opened the door wide, revealing a small, windowless, carpeted foyer.

"What's this?"

"The mayor's residence," he answered in a soft tone. "That way." He pointed to a hallway in front of them, leading to the main floor and public rooms. "I'm happy to give you an official tour."

Then he pointed to a small staircase at one side, his intense gaze locking on to hers. "That way is a shortcut to my private suite."

Under the spell of his blue eyes, her stomach did a free fall, memories of their lovemaking blooming in her mind, desire coalescing between her legs.

He waited, obviously letting her be the one to decide.

"Can we?" she whispered, half to him, half to herself, wondering if she dared.

"Totally up to you." He took her hand, wrapping it in his

strong fingers, bringing her knuckles to his lips for a gentle kiss.

How much worse could it get? she asked herself. They'd already made love twice. They were, for all intents and purposes, indulging in a clandestine fling. How could doing it once more change anything?

He reeled her in, placing the other arm around her waist, easing her against him. "What do you think?"

She nodded, slowly at first, then more decisively.

"Maverick," he muttered, a grin spreading across his face as he turned her for the staircase.

Decision made, they rushed up to the landing, coming to a hallway outside Seth's private door. He let them in, clicking it firmly shut behind them, immediately hauling her into his arms for a long, deep kiss. His hand held the back of her head, anchoring them together, while hot lips urged hers apart and his tongue plundered.

He pushed her blazer off her shoulders, tossing it aside. Then he stripped off her tank top, stopping the kiss only long enough to get the top over her head.

When he popped the button on her jeans, she kicked off her shoes. In a moment, she was naked, his warm palms running over her skin.

"I've missed you," he whispered, kissing her ear, her cheek, the crook of her neck. "I miss you all the time. I think about your scent. I think about your taste."

His forearm wrapped around the small of her back, pulling her tight, while he teased her nipple to a peak, eliciting a moan from deep in her throat. Her body was beginning to sing, her skin flush with reaction.

His kisses moved down her neck, to her shoulder, to her breast. His strong hands kneaded her bottom, and he moved lower and lower, kissing her belly, her navel.

"Seth," she hissed.

His breathing was ragged. "I'm sorry. I know this is too

fast. But I can't wait. I want to kiss every inch of your body. All of it. Right now."

His hands slid down her thighs, urging them apart. She braced her hands on his head. Soon, his kisses became excruciatingly intimate, and she dug her fingertips into his thick hair.

"It's not too fast," she assured him.

If anything, it was too slow. They'd spent too much time apart. She'd thought of him, dreamed of him, ached for him. Her legs began to tremble; she wasn't going to be able to stand much longer.

He rose, his eyes dark as midnight, scooping her into his arms and carrying her to the bedroom.

He deposited her on the thick four-poster bed, watching her with sheer animal possession as he stripped off his jacket and tie.

Arousal still shimmered through her body. She lay there naked, loving his gaze on her, loving the rushed determination as he took off his clothes. She reveled in the sight of his broad chest, muscular shoulders, rock-hard abs.

He, too, kicked off his shoes and stripped off his pants. In seconds he was naked, and she sat up, perching on the edge of the bed, reaching out to him, wrapping her hands around his solid body. She leaned forward, tasting the salt of his chest, his belly, farther downward until he gasped.

He braced his hands on her shoulders, easing her back onto the bed. Then he followed her down.

"Don't wait," she whispered to him, parting her thighs.

"You sure?"

"Now, please, now."

"With pleasure." He smoothly entered her body.

Her head tipped back, and she moaned with satisfaction as he filled her tight, sending hot tingles of pleasure from her belly to her toes. She kissed his mouth, squeezed him against her, lifting her hips to meet his long, hard thrusts.

Everything in her world disappeared. Nothing mattered but

Seth. Nothing existed but Seth. Her climax built and built to impossible heights, hovering on the brink, tearing his name from her lips, until a rush of light and sound catapulted her over the edge.

He called her name, but it seemed to echo down a tunnel, coming from a long way.

"Darby," he rasped again. "Darby, Darby, Darby."

His weight came down on top of her, pressing her warmly into the soft mattress. He twined his fingers with hers, holding her hands on either side of her head. He kissed her swollen, tender lips, softly, almost reverently.

"Are you okay?" he breathed on a rush.

"Good," she managed.

"I didn't hurt you?"

"Not that I noticed."

He raised himself up on his elbows, tracing a line from her shoulder to her belly. "Oh, man, I'm in big trouble here."

"Why?" she asked, with a quick glance around the room, wondering if they were caught.

"Not that kind of trouble." He smiled and brushed her messy hair back from her face. "I'm afraid that every night from here on in, I'm going to wish you were here."

She smiled at him. "That's a very sexy line."

He eased himself to her side, and she immediately missed his weight.

"It wasn't a line," he told her, a little edge to his voice.

She shifted to come up on one elbow. "I didn't mean it like that."

He met her gaze. "How did you mean it?"

"I meant it was a nice thing to say. A woman likes to think she'll be remembered."

"Darby, I didn't mean I'd remember you." He cupped her chin, gaze boring into hers. "I meant I'd ache for you."

"Okay, that one was even better. I was half afraid I was going to regret doing this again. But that's a line that'll keep a girl going for months."

He let his hand drop. "I have a feeling we're having two different conversations here."

"If you're saying we're fantastic together, then we're on exactly the same page."

His expression perked up. "You think we're fantastic together?"

She traced her own line down his chest and over his belly. "You, cowboy, know exactly what you're doing."

His lips curved up in a satisfied smile. "You want to do it again?"

"Absolutely."

Ten

Though his private suite didn't have a kitchen, Seth was able to find a tin of chocolate-covered blueberries and some California wine to stave off their hunger. Both had been gifts from the mayor of San Diego.

"Saddle broncs, maybe," he answered Darby's question. "But Travis still rides bulls."

"I've never even ridden a horse," she said.

She was sitting cross-legged on the bed, enveloped in his black robe. He'd pulled on his slacks and lit a couple of candles. The tin of blueberries sat half-empty between them, and they'd started on a second bottle of Napa Valley cabernet sauvignon.

"I could teach you," he offered.

"I don't know, Seth. A month from now, one of us is not going to be speaking to the other." She popped another dark-chocolate–covered blueberry into her mouth.

"You think it'll come to that?" He felt a twinge, thinking about Danielle down in Denver right now, and what was about to happen to Darby's hopes of winning.

"If you win, I'll be leaving Lyndon," she said.

He sat up abruptly. "Why?"

"The business will close. I'll have to sell out. The sale price will barely cover the outstanding mortgage, and I'll have nowhere to live."

Everything inside him balked at the idea of her leaving. It was frightening to think about why he felt that way.

"Of course, if *I* win, only good things happen," she continued.

"Sure. Except for the part where Lyndon loses the railway, and the part where I get kicked out of office." He was exaggerating for effect.

He reached for the wine bottle and polished it off between their glasses.

"I don't think they can impeach you for losing a referendum," Darby mused. "Though, I suppose you might not get re-elected next year."

Seth replaced the empty bottle on the bedside table. "I doubt I'll run for re-election."

"Seriously?" She looked up at him as she took a sip.

He hadn't told his family or his staff yet, but he was questioning the wisdom of having gone into politics in the first place.

"It's a frustrating job," he admitted.

For some reason he wanted to share with her in a way he hadn't with his family. Maybe it was because they were half-naked. Maybe it was the wine or the candlelight. Or maybe it was because she had shared some of her unguarded thoughts with him.

"Did you expect it to be easy?" she asked.

He was surprised by the challenge in her tone. "No."

"The most rewarding things in life are hard fought and hard-won."

"What makes you think I don't know that?"

"Because you're talking about quitting. I felt like quitting during basic training. I felt like quitting all the time. But I'm eternally glad that I did not."

"You eventually did quit the army," he pointed out, feeling slightly defensive. Maybe he shouldn't have shared his true feelings with her.

Her tone turned reflective, her expression less challenging. "Because I thought I could do more good on the outside."

"Bingo. I can't do what I expected to be able to do as mayor."

"Because of me?" There was a surprising look of guilt in her green eyes.

"If I say yes, will you give up the fight?"

She seemed to think about it for a moment. "If I believed you, I might."

He tried to put a wounded tone into his voice. "You don't believe me?"

"I don't believe you."

It was Seth's turn to think about it. "You're a very intelligent woman, Darby Carroll."

"You're probably just a bad liar."

"I thought mayors would concentrate on the big things, issues of strategic importance that could impact the citizens, change lives, improve the community. But it's the little stuff, the crazy-making stuff that sucks up all your time."

"Like what?" She leaned over to place her glass on the bedside table.

The robe fell open, baring one breast, and he realized he was hungry for her all over again. She was so indescribably beautiful, almost angelic. He could make love with her, talk with her, or simply sit here and gaze at her forever.

Forever.

The word echoed frighteningly through his mind. He didn't want Darby to leave, not tonight, not tomorrow. He'd never known another woman like her. He doubted another woman like her existed. And he wanted her all for himself.

"Seth?" she prompted. "What kind of crazy-making things?"

He gave himself a mental shake. "Barking dogs. Teenagers whooping it up in fast cars. Lawnmowers running too early in the morning or too late at night. There's a feud going on over on Baker Street over whether the owner of a certain tree should rake the leaves that fall in his neighbor's yard."

Darby laughed at that one.

"It gets worse," he warned. "In April, Mrs. Blackstone swears she saw an alien in her backyard. Her neighbor, Bert Campbell, thinks it was a Sasquatch. But both are now sleeping with their shotguns under their beds. The only thing that saves the neighborhood pets from certain death is the fact that neither of them can hit the broad side of a barn, and they both sleep like the dead."

"Can't you get out there and catch that alien?" Darby demanded.

"One night, Travis and I pretended to go on a Sasquatch hunt."

"Pretended?"

"We took along a case of beer and watched the Broncos game on my tablet out in the bush."

"You actually lied to a constituent about a Sasquatch hunt?"

"Through my teeth. I told him we saw footprints heading out over Beachnut Ridge." Seth shook his head as he recalled that night. "Figured we'd scared it off, and it was long gone. So the next day, the mayor's office got a call from strangethings.com. It seems they'd interviewed Bert Campbell, and he gave them my name to back up his story."

Darby burst out laughing.

"So you can see why I question the value of my contribution as mayor."

"So you'll go back to ranching?"

"I think so. I should find us something else to eat, or we're going to end up drunk and unable to drive." He rolled to his feet, thinking there had to be other edible gifts stored on the shelf of his front closet.

"I can take a cab home," said Darby.

He paused for a moment to gaze down at the picture she made on his bed, in his robe. "Or you can stay," he offered softly.

"Seth?" Travis's voice suddenly interrupted; the main door to the suite banged shut.

Seth swore under his breath, while Darby reflexively closed the robe.

"I'll be right out," Seth called.

"I thought we were meeting for a—" Travis appeared in the bedroom doorway, freezing to a halt when he spotted Darby. It obviously took him a split second to recognize her, but when he did, his expression darkened.

"What *the hell?*" he demanded.

"I told you I'd be right out," Seth snapped, moving to block his view of Darby and drive him back to the living room.

"Here?" Travis stood his ground, pointing at Darby. "Seriously, *here?*"

"It's none of your business," Seth told his brother.

"With everything that's going on?"

"Shut up," Seth ordered.

"You are *not* thinking straight."

"I'm thinking just fine," Seth retorted, even though he knew he was losing his mind over Darby.

Travis growled. "Do you honestly not know a conflict of interest when she's naked underneath you?"

Seth grabbed his brother by the collar and shoved him up against the wall.

The move obviously took Travis by surprise, because he didn't do anything to defend himself.

In Seth's peripheral vision, Darby came to her feet, tightening the belt of the robe.

"Apologize," Seth demanded of Travis.

"For pointing out the truth?"

"For being offensive and disrespectful."

"It's okay," Darby cut in, hovering beside the bed.

"No, it's not okay," said Seth. "Apologize *now*."

"I apologize," said Travis, tone flat, gaze never leaving Seth. "For being offensive and disrespectful."

"That lacked sincerity," said Seth.

"It's really okay," said Darby, taking a step forward.

"What are you *doing?*" asked Travis.

"This doesn't change a thing," Seth emphatically stated.

"It's true," Darby backed him up. "We've agreed it'll be a fair fight."

Travis shot Seth a look of renewed incredulity. "Fair?" he challenged. *"Fair?"*

Seth clenched his jaw, and the two men glared at each other.

"You can't blame him for being confused," Darby added, looking to Seth. "You and me doesn't make any sense."

"It makes perfect sense," said Seth.

"You're going to get hurt," Travis told Darby.

Seth took a long, deep breath. Travis knew Danielle was in Denver, trying to get the referendum canceled. He knew the railroad side was very likely to win, while Darby did not.

"Or Seth will get hurt," she retorted. "My side is doing *very* well."

Travis slid a censorious gaze to Seth.

Seth returned it with a warning stare. Luckily, Travis knew enough to keep his mouth shut. But he glanced around the room, taking in the wine bottles.

"You need a ride home?" he asked Darby.

"She's not leaving."

"She's going to stay for breakfast?" Travis demanded. "Meet the staff? Maybe walk you to your office? I've experienced the mood of this town. Do you have *any* idea what you're playing with here?"

Seth let go of his brother's shirt. He knew Travis was disappointed in him. And he understood why. But that didn't change the way he felt about Darby.

He wanted the railroad, but he wanted Darby, too. It didn't have to make sense. It didn't have to be easy. But he had to try.

"I'll get dressed," Darby said into the silence.

Seth turned to her, opening his mouth to talk her out of leaving.

"Travis is right," she told him firmly. "I can't stay."

"You can't go," Seth insisted.

"We've risked enough already," she returned.

"I'll be in the living room," Travis said, brushing past Seth.

Seth moved to where he was facing Darby. "Stay?" he asked her. "Stay a while longer."

She placed a hand on his chest. "You know I have to leave. People might have seen us come back here. It's plausible you've been giving me a tour of the mansion for the last couple of hours, but any longer, and people are going to figure it out."

"Figure what out?" he asked. That he'd fallen fast and hard for Darby?

"That one of us is trying to bribe the other with sex."

His stomach contracted. "Is that what we're doing?"

"I don't know what we're doing, Seth." She slid her hands up his bare chest to his shoulders. "I only know that it feels good, and I wish it didn't have to end."

"I'm telling you it doesn't have to end. Not right now. Not this second."

She came up on her toes and gave him a quick kiss. "Buck up, Mr. Mayor. Let your brother drive me home."

He longed to argue, but he knew she was right. Tonight couldn't happen. But he feared what would happen when Danielle got back with the state-level court decision.

Darby gave him a sad smile. "I know when to call for a strategic retreat. But we've got some time. It'll be weeks before we know who wins and who loses."

Seth's stomach went hollow again. "Right. I'll let you get dressed." He left the bedroom, heading down the hall to face his brother.

"Do you hate her?" Travis demanded quietly. "Are you that coldhearted that you'd use her that way?"

Seth let his indignation come through in his tone. "Of course I don't hate her."

"Then do you care about her?"

Seth didn't answer.

"How much?" Travis persisted.

"Too much."

"Well, then I feel sorry for you, bro. Because you're going to crash fast and hard."

"Maybe," Seth allowed. "But maybe not."

"I take it she doesn't know about your appeal to the state."

"Of course she doesn't know. Why would I tell her? Why would I compromise our position?"

"I don't know. Just off the top of my head, because *you're sleeping with her?*"

"I didn't tell her," Seth stated flatly.

"She thinks it's a fair fight."

"It is a fair fight."

Travis snorted. "She thinks she's getting a referendum."

"She knows I'm trying to stop it."

"She doesn't know you've succeeded."

"I haven't succeeded yet."

"Danielle's flying home tonight."

Seth stilled, everything inside him going cold. "She's done?"

"She's done. I just talked to Caleb. You won, big brother."

"That's great," Seth managed.

"You don't sound happy."

"I am happy."

"I'm ready to go," Darby called as she made her way down the short hallway.

"Don't you dare tell her," Seth growled to Travis.

"She's going to find out soon."

"Not tonight, she's not." Seth needed some time to think this through. And he simply couldn't stand the thought of upsetting Darby tonight.

"Under a hypothetical situation," Darby began as she parked her bag in the front closet and tugged off her shoes, after Travis had dropped her off.

"What hypothetical situation?" Marta looked up from her phone where she was reading email.

"The one where I slept with Seth to distract him from fighting with me on the referendum."

"Okay." She brushed her thumb across the screen, scrolling, and glanced back down.

"How badly would it go…" Darby took the opposite end of the couch. "If I fell for him?"

Marta shot Darby her full attention, eyes squinting down. "As in seriously, I-think-this-is-bigger-than-the-both-of-us fell for him?"

Darby slumped back in her seat. "Right."

"Uh-oh." Marta set her phone on the coffee table, turning sideways on the couch and drawing up her legs.

Darby copied Marta's posture, letting her mind go back over the evening. "He's just… I mean, he's intelligent, he's thoughtful, he's a lot more compassionate than I expected and he's funny."

"And sexy?"

The memories had the power to send heat coursing through Darby's system. "Oh, so incredibly sexy."

"So what are you going to do?" Marta asked softly.

Darby plucked at the wrinkled fabric of her slacks. "I'm trying to see a path forward. If I lose, I'm leaving. If he loses, you know, do you think he'd ever be able to get over it?"

She'd tried to imagine Seth getting past their fights, maybe coming to the conclusion that losing the railway wasn't the end of the world, maybe giving the two of them a chance. A chance to do what, she wasn't exactly sure. But she was sure she wanted what was between them to continue.

"A month is a long time," Marta responded. "If he's feeling it, too, he might get over the disappointment."

"He might," Darby agreed, trying not to let her hopes rise. "I never knew I could feel this way."

Marta considered her for another long moment. "Are you already in love with him?"

Darby emphatically shook her head. "I don't know him well enough to be in love."

Marta chuckled. "Is there a gauge of some kind?"

"Something between one and one hundred millibars," Darby joked in return.

Then her mind wandered off, trying to assign a number. Seventy? No, not enough. Maybe an eighty, or a glorious ninety.

Marta picked up her phone. "I bet there's an impartial quiz available that can help you decide. Maybe something by a women's magazine."

She clicked her way through the screens, while Darby tried to convince herself Seth wasn't already a hundred.

Then Marta's expression darkened, her eyes narrowing, lips going thin. "Uh-oh."

"Can't find a quiz?" Darby asked.

"I just got an email from one of our railway street team members."

Darby's mood took a downward turn. "Did something happen?"

"He heard from a friend in Denver, whose girlfriend works at the state courthouse. A decision came down today. It referenced Lyndon Valley and the railway referendum." Marta scrolled along the screens. "Crap!"

"What?" The pit of Darby's stomach convulsed.

"The city appealed the District Court's decision to the

State Court of Appeals." Marta looked up at her, expression grave. "They won."

Darby's nerves turned to fear. "What does that mean?" she asked slowly.

"The judge's decision to grant the referendum was declared void and thrown out. There's not going to be a referendum."

Darby shot her way down the length of the couch, peering over Marta's shoulder. "How can they do that? Why weren't we told?"

"Technically," said Marta, scanning the screen, "we weren't a party to the original decision."

"It was *our* petition."

"The petition didn't trigger the referendum. The judge decided that based on the mounting local protests."

"That's not fair." Darby removed the phone from Marta's hand and read her way through the brief article.

"Morally, no," Marta agreed. "Legally, yes."

"He went behind my back," Darby ground out.

"We'd have gone behind his," Marta replied.

"It says the decision came down at four o'clock today. That's before I met Seth at City Hall. The whole time, the *entire* time we were together tonight, he already knew it was over."

"Looks like he did," Marta agreed.

"He knew I'd lost," Darby continued, her anger building. "He knew I was leaving town, yet he—" She resisted an urge to throw Marta's phone across the room.

Obviously sensing her angry instinct, Marta pried Darby's fingers from her phone and tucked it away in her pocket.

"That's pretty stone-cold," said Marta.

"It's pretty stone-cold," Darby agreed.

Marta put a comforting hand on Darby's shoulder. "Maybe he's not, you know, exactly how he presented himself."

"You think he was acting all this time?" Darby couldn't

help but think back over their conversations, their lovemaking, his confession about not liking the mayor's role. Had they all been lies? Had she been a colossal fool?

"By romancing you, he kept you distracted," Marta pointed out.

Darby's anger was rapidly being replaced by mortification. There was a good chance Seth had played her. He'd played her better than she could ever have hoped to play him.

"I agreed to tone down the rhetoric," she stated in self-disgust. "Was it all part of his master plan? Keep me busy, keep me distracted, all the while coming at it from the state level?"

"With no more public protests, there was no reason for the court not to overturn. He's good." Marta's tone was laced with reluctant admiration.

"He beat us," Darby said.

"Because we underestimated him," Marta said, obviously going deep into thought.

"Is there anything we can do?" Darby asked, a small measure of hope coming up at the calculating expression on Marta's face. "Can we appeal the appeal?"

"We can't," said Marta. "Without the referendum, the permits all become instantly valid. He's already expropriated your land. I think they can start building the railroad tomorrow."

Darby's entire body slumped. "We lost. And I was completely taken in by a con artist."

"If it makes you feel any better, I think he's a world-class con artist."

"It doesn't make me feel any better."

Darby was heartsick. She was about to lose Sierra Hotel. There was never going to be anything between her and Seth. The magical evening they'd just shared had been an illusion.

Who knew how many lies he'd told. While he was stroking her cheek and kissing her mouth, he was probably thinking about all the money his family would make shipping cattle on the railroad.

She'd given herself to him—completely, freely, honestly. She'd let him past every defense she had, and he'd been faking his feelings the entire time. He'd only run for mayor to help his community? He didn't get a chance to focus on the big issues? He might not even run again? Ha!

He'd brought this big issue home in a way that absolutely guaranteed his re-election.

"I feel like an idiot," she whispered to Marta.

Marta gave a heartfelt sigh. "It turns out you're too trusting for your own good."

"I never wanted to be trusting. I wanted to be tough. I wanted to be smart, and I wanted to be realistic."

"You're all of those things."

"Not when it counts."

"This is a big loss," Marta agreed, in the usual no-nonsense tone that Darby had always admired. "But it's done."

Darby forced herself to square her shoulders. "It's done."

"Nobody died."

"Nobody died," Darby agreed. Only her hopes and dreams....

Marta wrapped an arm around her shoulder and squeezed tight. "We learn from our mistakes, and we soldier on."

Darby gave a sharp nod.

"Maybe you replace Sierra Hotel somewhere else," Marta continued.

"I can't afford to replace it." Darby was going to have to sell. She'd have to sell before construction started and she lost all of her customers and her income.

"Or maybe there's something else in your future, something exciting, meaningful and positive."

"I could reenlist," Darby speculated.

Private psychology practice in an office didn't appeal to her. And there were certainly plenty of women on the front lines who could use her help.

"They would take you back in a heartbeat," Marta agreed.

"I'm not going to let him know he did this," Darby stated with determination. "He might have played me better, but he'll never know I wasn't playing, too."

"That a girl." Marta approved.

"Rat bastard."

"That a girl," Marta repeated with conviction.

Eleven

Seth had waited three days to hear from Darby. At first, he'd hoped she would forgive him. Then he hoped she'd at least come yell at him. Then he wondered if maybe he should make the first move. In the end, he began to fear he should have made the first move three days ago.

He hadn't wanted to gloat, he'd rationalized. And she'd never been one to keep her thoughts to herself. It had been perfectly reasonable for him to expect her to show up when she was ready to have it out.

He wasn't sorry he'd won. It was the best thing for the town, and Lyndon was definitely in a celebratory mood over the decision. The detractors had either changed their minds or were keeping a low profile now that the deal was done.

The Mountain Railway brass were in town today for both a celebration and a ribbon-cutting ceremony. The press would be out in force, and there would be photo ops along with a formal thank-you to the mayor for making the project possible. Finally, it was Seth's big moment. He'd done what he'd set out to do two years ago. He'd succeeded. He'd made a difference in the town and in the entire Valley.

Construction would start in the spring, but a lot of the detailed surveying and planning work could take place over the winter.

For now, he tied the bow tie on his tux, glancing at his watch while a regional news show played in the background. He was hosting a VIP dinner at the town hall tonight after the press conference, thanking Mountain Railway and welcoming the senior construction managers to the city.

If he didn't hear from Darby tonight, he decided, he'd head up to Sierra Hotel in the morning. Or maybe the dinner would break up early, and he could drive up tonight.

Sure, they were adversaries. But he thought she'd understood the rules. He knew she'd understood the rules. If she'd had the same chance as him to win fair and square, she'd have taken it in a heartbeat. She'd have to admit that. She'd also have to admit that they couldn't simply walk away from what they'd shared in his bed.

He blew the bow tie knot once more, swore out loud and started over.

His suite door opened.

"They're fifteen minutes away," said Travis. "You need to get down to the receiving line."

"I'll be ready," Seth confirmed, fumbling and swearing once again.

"You need help?" Travis asked.

"I'm not in high school." Seth forced himself to slow down and concentrate.

"You heard from Darby?"

"No."

"You call her?"

"No."

Travis didn't even attempt to hide his mocking tone. "You haven't even tried to apologize?"

"Back off." Seth didn't need another condemning voice inside his head.

"I don't believe I will back off. You've been storming around here like a wounded grizzly bear for three days, when you should be celebrating with everyone else. It's confusing for the citizens."

"I *am* celebrating," Seth insisted. "I'm posing for pictures. I'm making speeches. I'm toasting with champagne. Look at this. I'm dressing up in a *tux,* for God's sake."

"And you seem genuinely thrilled about it."

Seth finally got the tie right. "I am genuinely thrilled about it. I won. She lost. The woman is going to have to deal with it."

"You should tell it to her exactly like that."

Seth turned to glare at his brother.

"Or maybe you should beg her to forgive you for being such an ass."

"I wasn't an ass. I'm not going to apologize for winning."

"You should apologize for sleeping with her while keeping her in the dark about the appeals court," said Travis.

"It would have been a conflict of interest for me to tell her."

"You could have kept your hands to yourself."

Seth knew he could have, he should have. Would things be better right now if he had?

"Do you think she'd like me to apologize?" he found himself asking.

"It might be too late."

Seth stilled. "What do you mean?"

"I mean, she's put the place up for sale. Listed it today."

Seth gave Travis his complete attention. "How do you know that?"

"Abigail talked to her."

"When did she and Abigail become friends?"

"I don't know," said Travis. "But I do know that Darby is selling, and she's thinking about reenlisting."

Seth gave his head a little shake. "Repeat that last part."

Travis gave a pitying shake of his head. "I thought Abigail

might call you. Turns out, Sierra Hotel wasn't a ladies' retreat. It was a place for female service members and law-enforcement personnel who endure high-risk, high-stress jobs to get a little R & R with their peers before they go back to risking their lives in defense of their country or their community."

Seth reached out to grasp the back of a chair, several things coming clear to him all at once. The most important of which was that Darby might reenlist.

"She once told me the women came there to get away from loud, sudden noises."

"I imagine they did," said Travis.

"I accused them of having delicate sensibilities."

"Well," Travis responded. "I doubt that part is true."

"Why didn't she say something?"

"Would it have changed your mind?"

Seth knew it wouldn't have. What was right for Lyndon Valley was still right for Lyndon Valley. Though he was sorry it ruined Sierra Hotel.

"Tell me she hasn't reenlisted yet."

"Not that I know of."

"I have to go talk to her. Right now. Right this second."

Seth had to go now. Lyndon City and the Mountain Railway brass would simply have to live without him for tonight.

"Why now?" asked Travis.

"What do you mean, 'why now?' The woman's about to *rejoin the army.*"

It would take her away from Lyndon Valley for years, probably forever. And it would take her away from Seth. And Seth realized he couldn't let her go.

"So? That won't stop you from apologizing," Travis pressed.

Seth stopped cold.

His heart was beating hard in his chest. He could feel the adrenaline coursing through his system. Every instinct he had told him to take action. Every instinct he had told him to stop Darby from walking out of his life.

"I don't want her to go," he answered lamely.

Travis took a step toward him. "And what do you expect to do with her if she stays?"

It felt like a trick question to Seth. The quick answer was hold her hostage in his bed for about the next year. But he knew it wasn't that simple. He also realized what Travis was getting at.

"I don't want to hurt Darby. I don't want to cause her one minute of pain." As he said the words, Seth couldn't help but wonder how long they'd been true. They were *so* true.

"Then you better make up your mind exactly what you want from her. And do it before you talk to her."

"I know what I want from her," Seth confirmed.

He wanted her to love him back. He wanted her to agree to put this mess behind them. He wanted her to figure out the rest of her life in a way that included him.

"Good." Travis gave a sharp nod. "I'll help entertain the Mountain Railway people. You go see Darby before she faxes new enlistment papers to the recruiting office."

Darby hadn't decided for certain that she wanted to re-enlist, but it was definitely at the top of her options list. She planned to sell the furnishings and equipment, even the linens and dishes with Sierra Hotel. Whether back to the army, or on to someplace else, when she left Lyndon Valley at the end of the month, she'd be traveling light.

In her office, she taped up a box of paper records for the business. Everything was backed up electronically, but the originals she'd put in storage in a facility in Denver. She also had some books and photographs she wouldn't need right away, and there were a few of her great-aunt's possessions that she'd keep forever. Everything but her day-to-day essentials could be stored until she had a place of her own at some point in the future.

She wouldn't keep a single memento of Seth. Not that she had anything to keep. But if she did, she wouldn't want it.

She'd been struggling for days not to think about him, because every time her mind went in his direction, she felt as if her heart was being crushed inside her chest.

Deep down, she was forced to accept that the man she'd fallen in love with didn't really exist. But he'd seemed so real at the time. He'd seemed so incredibly real that her subconscious didn't want to let go of the fantasy.

At night, she dreamed about him, waking up alone and upset, aggravated by her overwhelming longing to hear his voice once again and to feel his body pressed up against hers.

He was gone.

It was done.

She was stronger than this.

"Darby?"

She whirled around at the sound of his voice, half expecting him to be an illusion.

He wasn't. He was standing in the doorway of her office, looking as sexy and handsome as ever in a tux, causing her heart to thud in her chest and her traitorous body to lurch involuntarily toward him. She stopped herself just in time.

"What are you doing here?" she asked, proud of her even, dispassionate tone. There was no way in the world she was going to let him see how badly he'd hurt her.

He took a pace into the room. "I thought we could talk."

"About what?" And why here? Not here. The first time they'd made love was in this room.

"The same thing we've been talking about for the past few weeks."

She looked him up and down, struggling hard to keep her expression from giving away how desperately she'd missed him. "There's nothing left to talk about. You won, I lost, game over."

He moved closer still. "Darby."

"Stay right where you are, Seth. I didn't invite you to come in."

He stopped. "I didn't mean to hurt you."

She folded her arms across her chest. "What makes you think you hurt me?"

He glanced around the room. "I know how much this place means to you."

She gave an unconcerned shrug. "Spoils of war. I'll start over someplace else."

"Is that a military metaphor?"

"I think it's in the general lexicon. Why are you here?"

Every second he stayed, she felt herself winding tighter and tighter. He'd hurt her. He'd hurt her badly. But she still had her pride. She would not let him see her break down.

He took one step closer. They were only about six feet apart.

"That last night," he said.

"You mean the night you duped me?" She gritted her teeth, willing herself not to remember even a moment of that night.

"I didn't know," he said.

"Didn't know what?"

"That Danielle had succeeded. That we'd won the appeal."

His assertion seemed like a ridiculous splitting of hairs. Her arms dropped back to her sides, and her hands clenched into fists.

"But you knew there *was* an appeal," she accused.

"Yes," he admitted.

"And you expected to win."

He nodded.

"Yet you pretended it was still a fair fight. That we had weeks." She stopped for a moment, fearing her voice would crack. "That one of us was going to win based on the referendum."

He didn't answer.

"You used sex to distract me."

Seth opened his mouth to speak.

She didn't let him. "I did that, too, Seth. There's no need to apologize. I used every weapon in my arsenal to defeat you, and I wouldn't have been sorry if I'd won."

"I'm not sorry I won," he allowed. "I am sorry you lost."

She scoffed out a laugh. "You can't have it both ways."

"Travis told me about Sierra Hotel."

"What about it?"

"What you do. The women you serve. Their duty and sacrifice."

Abigail had obviously told Travis. It didn't matter. There was no secret left to keep.

"It's a loss to the country," Seth said.

"It's none of your business. Seriously, Seth. You need to go now. We're done. Everything between us is done."

"Everything?" he asked, with yet another step toward her.

"Everything," she assured him, fighting an urge to fall back, then fighting an even stronger urge to rush forward.

As she'd asked herself the night in the mayor's mansion, a tiny, rebellious part of her brain wondered how much harm it would do to kiss him once more, maybe even sleep with him once more. It would be a chance to say goodbye.

She thought she saw a flash of pain cross his expression. But he quickly neutralized it.

"So that's all there was?" he asked. "The fight? It was the only thing ever between us?"

"What else would there have been?" she managed airily, her stomach clenching with the effort and her chest hollowing out.

"We made love, Darby."

"That was sex, Seth."

"Right." His jaw tightened, and his blue eyes went hard. "You only slept with me to distract me."

"I believe I made that perfectly clear at the time."

Why, oh, why didn't he leave? She didn't know how much longer she could keep this up.

"And nothing changed?" he pressed.

"Did anything change for you?" she challenged. "Between the time I first confronted you to the time you went to the appeal court without telling me, did something change? Did you ever stop and think maybe I was right and you were wrong?"

"I wasn't wrong," he said.

"You weren't," she agreed with finality. "You did what was right for Lyndon, and you can sleep well tonight. I was collateral damage, and I accept that, but you don't need to stand there and gloat. Now I'm asking you to leave my house. Please go."

She reached across the desk for another cardboard box, pressing open the flaps, and blindly grabbing the nearest stack of books to place inside.

He was silent for a long moment. When he spoke, there was a hollow tone to his voice. "Goodbye, Darby."

She didn't look up. "Goodbye, Seth."

Seth stopped on Darby's front porch, gripping the post at the top of the stairs and closing his eyes as a wave of anguish and regret washed over him. He remembered her sassy jokes, their passionate kisses and how on that last night, they'd made it past each other's defenses to their hopes and fears. He had to believe those were Darby's true hopes and fears. He couldn't imagine she'd been faking everything.

Marta's voice broke through the jumble of his thoughts. "I'm not sure you're as much of a jerk as you appear."

He opened his eyes to see her standing at the bottom of the staircase, feet planted apart, hands on her hips, late-afternoon sun hanging in the sky behind her.

"Is that supposed to be a compliment?" he asked.

"You played your hand very well."

"I'm not sure about that one, either," he responded. "Compliment?"

"Actually, it is. I'd have done the same thing you did. But what I don't get is the sex."

He couldn't figure out where she was going. "What's not to get? It was sex."

"Darby flirting with you, now that was a tactical maneuver, put you off balance, maybe let your guard down and give her some valuable information. But you actually having sex with her as a tactical maneuver. Well, you're either a coldhearted son of a bitch who used her for nothing more than physical gratification…"

Seth felt his blood pressure go up.

"Or," Marta continued, tone laced with speculation, "you had actual feelings for her."

"I'm not a coldhearted son of a bitch."

Marta smiled. "That's what I thought. You know what she's going to do."

"Reenlist."

"That's right. So if you can think of a single thing you can do to fix this, I'd suggest you do it. And you'd better do it now."

Seth was afraid to speculate on Marta's motives, what Darby might have confided in her. He didn't dare let himself start to hope.

"Why are you telling me this?" he asked, pleading inside that she'd give him something positive to go on.

"Like I said, I don't think you're as much of a jerk as you seem."

"Did Darby say something about me?"

"That's not a question I can answer."

"Did she hint she might care about me?" he pressed harder.

"I can't answer that, either. I can tell you, though, that while some women might sleep with a man solely for the purpose of manipulating him, I'd be shocked to my toes if Darby could pull it off."

That was good enough for Seth. Marta obviously had reason to believe Darby cared about him. He turned on his heel, deciding it was time for a last-ditch change in tactics.

Darby hadn't expected the overwhelming rush of despair that had enveloped her as soon as Seth left the inn. She'd been coping with anger, even loneliness for the past few days. But right now she felt like she was under water, as if the sunlight and oxygen had been sucked out of her world.

She swiped at a tear with the back of her hand, telling herself she wasn't going to do this. No man would ever have the power to hurt her this way. She was tough, and she knew how to fight, and she would not let her own emotions defeat her.

She heard footsteps and felt relieved to know Marta was back. It was nearly five, not too early to blend a batch of margaritas. What she needed right now was a stiff drink, a tub of gourmet ice cream and a good friend. They'd talk it out, and in the morning the world would look brighter.

Maybe.

Darby honestly couldn't picture that quite yet.

"Darby?"

Seth. Her stomach contracted in on itself.

"Darby?" he repeated.

She struggled to put on a brave face, praying no trace of her tears remained.

Gritting her teeth, she turned. "Did you forget something?"

A strange expression crossed his face. "Yeah, I did."

"What?"

He moved straight across the room to stand in front of her. His expression turned to uncertainty. "I'm not going to ask you how you feel."

"I feel fine," she lied.

"Because that would be unfair," he continued as if she hadn't spoken. "But here's what I want to say. If I elicit nothing in you, if your emotions flatline around me, then I'll walk out of your life and never come back."

Darby tried to tell him to go. She tried to force out the words that would take him from her life forever, but she couldn't seem to make a single sound.

"But if you feel something, anything—confusion, frustration, longing, loneliness or even anger—then I want to show you something."

"Show me what?"

A half smile grew on his face, and she knew she'd given too much away. She felt frustration. She felt confusion. She felt longing. And she sure felt anger.

"Come with me," he told her softly, moving toward her. "Right now. I want to show you something. It's important."

"No." She couldn't do it. How could she do it? How could she risk feeling even worse than she felt right now?

"Please," he asked her, every nuance of his expression, every note in his voice radiating sincerity.

She was so tempted, and she was so frightened by being so tempted.

"I feel like crap," he told her. "I can't do it. I can't let it end like this."

"It was always going to end like this."

He reached out and took her hands in his. "It never should have."

She felt tears burning at the back of her eyes. "I can't, Seth."

He unexpectedly smiled. "It's not a flatline, is it?"

Her heart thumped in her chest.

"It's not a flatline," she whispered, pained.

He squeezed one of her hands in his, turning and towing her toward the door. "Then let's go."

"No, Seth." She ordered herself to pull away, but his hand was so warm and strong around hers, that she couldn't quite bring herself to break the hold.

"It won't take long," he promised.

"Where are we going?" She realized the question was as good as agreeing.

"Down the valley. I need to show you something."

She stopped arguing, and she kept walking. She realized she wasn't strong enough to tell him no. She wasn't strong enough to give up this tiny chance to spend a few more minutes or hours with him.

They made their way to his pickup truck. They got silently inside. She fastened the seat belt over her hips, while he pointed the vehicle for the highway. A few minutes in, he tuned in a local station to fill the uncomfortable silence.

Darby wished she could come up with some small talk. But she couldn't think of a single thing to say. The questions that burned in her mind were way beyond small talk. What was he doing? Where were they going? What could he possibly say or do to alleviate her heartbreak and the destruction of her life?

Finally, she gave up. She tipped her head back and closed her eyes. Her chest didn't ache quite as much as it had the past few days. Even though she knew it was temporary, and he'd be leaving her again soon, his presence seemed to give her heartbreak a breather.

Two hours later, as the sun was setting, they passed beneath the Jacobs Ranch sign. Darby sat up straighter while they bumped their way up the long ranch road. She gazed out at the lush fields dotted with cattle, the river, the colored maple trees and the magnificent mountains rising beyond the Valley. She'd never been to his family ranch before.

"Your place?" she couldn't help confirming.

"That's right."

"Are we going to see your family?"

She glanced down at her tattered jeans and faded T-shirt. She really wasn't prepared to talk to anyone right now.

"No," he answered.

She breathed a sigh of relief, watching the sights once more. She'd heard people say it was the most beautiful ranch in the Valley, and she could easily see why.

"Will you tell me what we're doing?" she asked.

"Not yet. I want it to be a surprise."

Darby couldn't imagine what kind of a surprise would be at his ranch. "A horse?" she found herself guessing, though she was far from in the mood for humor. "A cow? A chicken?"

"Yeah," he drawled sarcastically. "I brought you out here to see a chicken."

"It's a beautiful ranch," she told him, the tension in her stomach easing a little more.

They were headed uphill, over faint tire tracks that crossed a sloping meadow. A picturesque lake fanned out in the twilight.

"I've always loved it," he replied, bringing the truck to a halt, shutting down the engine and setting the brake. "Here we are."

"So you wanted to show me a lake."

"Yeah." He smiled, opening the driver's door.

Darby followed suit as he rounded the hood.

"I don't understand, Seth."

"You will."

"I feel something," she told him. "I'm hurt and I'm angry, and I'm afraid you're making it worse."

"I have no intention of making it worse."

"I feel like everything is lies. I never should have slept with you."

Seth looked genuinely regretful. "I thought you'd come and yell at me. I was okay with you getting angry. I wasn't okay with you getting hurt."

"Then you shouldn't have betrayed me."

He closed his eyes for a long moment. "Oh, Darby. I am so sorry." His sincerity was clearly obvious.

"Thank you for that."

Then he took her hand. "This way."

She tried to hang on to her anger as they strolled through the meadow, but his apology had pricked her resolve. And there was something soothing about the smell of the fields, the fresh breeze in her hair and Seth's solid presence beside her.

She tried to brace herself for even more hurt when this final interlude was over.

"There it is," he said, and she looked up.

They had stopped in front of an overgrown homesite. She could see a potbellied stove, a crumbling chimney and the barest remnants of a small foundation. It took less than a second for her to realize where they'd come, remembering the view from the painting.

"It's your great-great-grandparents'," she muttered in wonder.

"This is the place."

She had no idea why he'd brought her here, but she felt inordinately grateful. It was almost sacred ground. She could feel the roots of his family through the soles of her shoes.

"It's even better than the painting," she told him, dropping her hand from his, moving forward, trying to picture the family living here years and years ago.

"You like it?" he asked.

"I still agree with Mandy. Someone should carry on the family on this site."

"Well, carry on something," he said. He walked up behind her, putting his hands on her shoulders.

"I was thinking, after Travis told me about Sierra Hotel, that this would be a perfect spot to rebuild it."

Darby's insides turned to stone. She twisted her head to gape at him. Was he suggesting his family could replace Sierra Hotel? That somebody else should take her idea and run with it?

"I was thinking," he continued softly, not reacting to her incredulous expression. "If you were to marry me, we could rebuild Sierra Hotel right here on the ranch."

Her jaw dropped.

"What do you think?"

"What?" she rasped, wondering if she could have possibly heard right. He was proposing? How could he possibly be proposing?

"I think you heard me," he said.

"That is by far the craziest thing you've ever said."

"Which part is the craziest?" He turned her to face him. "Me offering to replace Sierra Hotel so that you'll marry me? Or you agreeing to marry me so that I'll replace Sierra Hotel?"

"Seth, *what* is going on?"

He took both her hands in his and gently squeezed, sending sparks of desire up her arms to her heart. "I'm in love with you, Darby. That's what's going on. I'm head over heels in love with you, and I can't bear the thought of losing you. I can't stand that I've hurt you." His gaze went past her shoulder to the small homesite. "I know it's second best. It's not your aunt's place. But I want you to carry on with Sierra Hotel. I want—"

"Whoa," Darby interrupted him, her mind reeling in amazement and confusion. "Go back."

His expression fell. "You want to leave?"

"Go back to the part where you said you love me."

His shoulders sagged in relief, and the smile returned to his face. "I love you, Darby. Will you marry me?"

"This is too fast," she protested, her heart pounding and joy coming to life deep inside her.

"I don't know how to slow it down. I can't let you leave. I can't let you rejoin the army."

Logic told her to be cautious, but her emotions were already shouting from the rooftops.

"It's all too unbelievable," she told him.

"What can I do to make it more believable?"

"I don't know. Kiss me or something."

A wide smile brightened his face. He drew her gently into his arms, bringing his lips down on hers in an exquisitely tender kiss that went on and on.

Darby's heart sang with happiness. She clung tightly to him, every fiber of her being telling her this was where she belonged.

"I love you," she whispered against his mouth. "I'll marry you, Seth."

He lifted her right up off the ground, twirling her in the air, kissing her all over again.

"How soon?" he asked.

Epilogue

Darby had never expected to have a big wedding. But when the mayor got married, there was a very long list of must-invite people. So they took their vows in the city's largest church, then used every square inch of the mayor's mansion's public area for the reception, including a big, heated tent on the grounds for dancing.

Darby met Seth's parents, who welcomed her into the family with open arms. They seemed genuinely thrilled to learn about Sierra Hotel, and agreed that the old homesite was the perfect spot to build.

Marta was maid of honor, while Travis was best man. Darby wore a simple, off the shoulder, white silk dress, with a slender, full-length skirt. Her neck was adorned with a diamond-and-sapphire necklace that Seth had presented her with the night before. It matched her custom-designed engagement ring.

Sawyer hovered over the now very pregnant Abigail. Katrina was a vision in frills and lace, while Mandy had gone for a basic burgundy cocktail dress. Still, her husband Caleb had hungrily watched her every move.

Travis gave a funny, heartfelt toast. And then he was the life of the dance, until Danielle slapped his face.

Darby had wondered if they should step in and break up the fight. But Seth had just laughed and said his brother could take care of himself. It hadn't been Travis whom Darby was worried about, but one look at Danielle's expression told Darby nobody was going to mess with her.

They'd gone with French vanilla cake and buttercream icing. It was eminently edible, and Darby had enjoyed every last bite. For a formal event, it had become very laid back and fun as the night wore on.

Finally, Seth had escorted a very happy but tired Darby upstairs to the mayor's private suite. He pushed open the door and lifted her into his arms.

Darby couldn't help but laugh. "I feel like a princess."

"You're supposed to feel like a princess," he rumbled in her ear.

"I never expected to have anything remotely like this for a wedding." Then her eyes focused on the living room, seeing the fire, the candles and a table set for two with a white linen cloth, flowers, hors d'oeuvres and a bottle of champagne. "Oh, Seth."

"For my bride," he whispered, setting her down. "I thought you might be hungry."

"I am," she agreed. "It's been a long night."

"You want to slip into something more comfortable?"

"I'd like that." Her dress was beautiful, but a little tight, and the stays in the bodice were digging into her ribs.

There was a glimmer in his eyes. "I put something out on the bed that I think you might like."

She grinned. "That I might like, or that you might like?"

"Oh, I'll like it a lot," he admitted.

She stroked his cheek with her palm. "One wedding-night ensemble, coming up."

"I'll open the champagne," he called as she walked away.

Moving to the bedroom, she pulled the pins and flowers out of her hair, letting it fall around her shoulders. She reached around to the zipper, sighing as the tight bodice fell away. Then she stepped out of the dress and hung it in the closet.

When she looked at the bed, she burst out laughing. She'd expected satin and lace, something short and naughty. What she got was a blue tank top and a pair of gray sweatpants.

She returned to the living room and did a pirouette in front of Seth.

"You opted for comfortable?" she asked.

"Are you comfortable?" he returned.

"Completely."

"Good." He handed her a glass of champagne. He had stripped down to his slacks and dress shirt, rolling up the sleeves. "Tonight's about you, not about me. I think you're beautiful in anything.

"Plus—" he clinked their two glasses together "—I'm planning to take it off you later, anyway."

"I love you, Seth," she told him before sipping the sweet, bubbly liquid.

"I adore you, Darby. Mrs. Jacobs." His tone went husky, and his arm slipped around her waist. "My wife."

He gave her a kiss. "I have one more present for you."

She drew back. "What? Are you kidding? I didn't get you anything."

"You've already given me everything. There's nothing else I need."

"But that's not fair," she protested, even as he extracted a long, cardboard tube from the corner desk.

He handed it to her with a flourish.

"It's not even wrapped," she joked.

"How soon you get spoiled."

She bopped him gently on the head with the tube, and he laughed. Then she pried off the plastic end and peered into the darkness. "What is it?"

"Architectural drawings." He pulled out several large sheets of paper. "Three options for Sierra Hotel. If you like one of them, we can break ground tomorrow."

"Seriously?" she asked, crossing to the desk where they could roll the plans out.

"If we pour the foundation before freeze-up, the contractor can work all winter. By the time construction starts on the railway in the spring, you'll have a whole new home."

She paged through the drawings, liking all of them.

"You didn't have to do this," she told him in awe.

"I did," he responded, stroking her hair. "It's my fault you lost your family home."

"I have a new family home. And a new family."

"You do." He kissed the delicate spot beside her ear. "You'll never be alone again."

* * * * *

If you loved A COWBOY'S TEMPTATION,
don't miss a single COLORADO CATTLE BARONS *novel:*
A COWBOY COMES HOME
A COWBOY IN MANHATTAN
AN INTIMATE BARGAIN
MILLIONAIRE IN A STETSON
A COWBOY'S TEMPTATION

All available now from
USA TODAY *bestselling author Barbara Dunlop*
and Harlequin Desire!